3

HOLES IN THE SKY

A NOVEL BY

MARK REPS

Copyright © 201 Mark Reps
All rights reserved.
ISBN: 10: 1490938303
ISBN-13: 978-1490938301

D1713203

DEDICATION

This book is dedicated to my wife, Kathy, for her steadfast belief in all that I attempt. It is further dedicated to all of my readers. I humbly thank you.

I would especially like to thank Elsa Biel Wilkie for her tremendous work editing HOLES IN THE SKY. Her attention to detail is simply amazing.

This book is a work of fiction. Names and characters are products of the author's imagination. Any similarities between the good people of Safford, AZ and tribal members of the San Carlos Indian Reservation are purely coincidental.

The background of the story, however, is partially based in truth. Mount Graham is a real place and a sacred site of the Apache Nation. There has been a long standing and contentious battle between the US Government and the Apache Nation as to ownership and usage of Mount Graham. The Apache Nation believes the telescopes on Mount Graham infringe upon their religious freedom, a constitutional right, and that the improper land usage imposes a threat to their cultural survival. Legal battles involving the Apache Survival Coalition and numerous environmental groups against the principals involved have been ongoing since 1988.

CHAPTER ONE

Under the dimly lit sky an effeminate hand gripped the shoulder of a nearly flaccid body and shook with unseeming strength. The clearing of a throat echoed in the otherwise silent night.

"You're still with me, aren't you, Padre? Padre!?"

The man, dressed in the collar of a Catholic priest, remained slumped over in the front seat of his station wagon. His nearly lifeless, drooling lips pressed against the passenger window. His eyes stared mindlessly into a rapidly approaching oblivion. Any semblance of voluntary control was rapidly ebbing into an unholy blackness from which death could be his only escape.

"Last rites, Padre...Extreme Unction...how does the sound of that ring in your ears?

The religious man dug deeply into the last vestiges of his manhood. A vain attempt to curse his captor barely exuded from his dying lips.

With a stronger, more confident air the captor spoke again. "Say that again, would you, Padre. I couldn't quite make it out."

A wheezing grunt oozed through his lips.

"Jesus sheds not a tear for a dying fool headed for hell."

The dying priest's stomach spasmed. A curdled glob of black and green fluid escaped unceremoniously through his flared nostrils. The driver shook his head in revulsion.

"Keep it together, Father. You're beginning to disgust me."

The watering eyes of the man in the collar disappeared somewhere deep into the back of his skull.

"What time frame does canon law prescribe as proper for the final sacrament?"

The sorrowful echo of the priest's unintelligible, dying voice volleyed around the inside of the car. The driver, stirred by its eeriness, grabbed the holy man by the collar and jerked him upright.

"Now listen up, Padre. About my religious-legal inquiry? Must Last Rites be administered within an hour of death? Or must the sacrament be administered prior to passing? If memory serves me correctly, I believe tradition demands the anointment of the dying must be administered before the soul departs the body. One of the great philosophical questions of all time, eh, Padre? Padre?"

The priest, held upright by a seatbelt, slumped limply forward in his seat. The man behind the wheel reached over, snatched him roughly by the hair and growled his question sternly.

"When precisely does the soul exit the body? Can you feel it leaving your body? More importantly, can you sense the direction it's heading? Tell me, Padre, is your soul going to heaven or is it going to meet its doom in oblivion?

If I were a gambler, I would put my money on hell."

The priest's strength had vanished. He could not even stir.

"Certainly the wise men in Rome who govern the Church have issued an edict or two on the subject."

The priest's corporal body collapsed into its final survival mode. He now breathed only the rasp of death.

"What? Speak up. You haven't answered my question. Maybe you don't have the answer? Don't worry. You will soon enough."

The driver pulled the car off the smooth pavement into a low wash. He parked behind a thicket of scraggly scrub brush and switched off the engine. Reaching over, he grabbed the priest's shoulder and shook him violently. When the holy man failed to respond, the driver reached into the glove compartment. He removed a small vial. It was labeled 'Holy Water, Saint Barnabus Church'. The driver took a swallow, tipped his head back and gargled before spitting the liquid onto the face of the dying man. The barely conscious priest managed a small gurgle through purplish-blue, foam-covered lips.

"Stay with me now, palsy-walsy. The best, as they say, is yet to come. Where is your God now, Padre? Hiding in the bushes? Waiting to save you? Why don't you have a little look around? Maybe you can find Him for me."

The driver grabbed the priest and twisted his neck, giving him a complete scan of the surrounding area.

"Nope, I don't think so. Your Savior has left you on your own. God Almighty has abandoned you in your time of need. Irony? Fate? Your call, Padre."

The driver released the priest's neck from his grip. From behind the seat he extracted a pair of neatly folded surgical gloves and a miner's hat. He methodically checked the brightness of the hat's lamp before forcing it tightly on his head. Finger by finger he tightened the gloves snugly around his smooth, uncalloused hands.

"Now don't go away, Padre. I'll be right back. I promise."

The man hopped out of the priest's station wagon. He lowered the back gate and grabbed the legs of a rocking chair. He grunted as he tugged hard on the wooden legs of the chair. The chair smacked clumsily onto the ground. The man's eyes and ears suddenly tuned in to the surrounding night. Assured no one was approaching, he flicked on the helmet's light. He grabbed the rocker and fought clumsily through the underbrush. When he reached a previously chosen spot in the ditch, he relieved himself of the burden. He took a moment to catch his breath as he squinted long and hard down the vanishing roadway. Confident he was alone, he ambled back to the car. He shouldered his prey using the adrenaline surge that comes with the power of death over life.

"I hope you're easier to wrangle than that goddamned rocker of yours."

The dying priest's stench-filled breath echoed shallowly in his captor's ear.

"What's that?" asked the man. "You're slurring your speech. Speak clearly if you expect to be spoken to."

Suddenly a rustling froze him like stone. It was only a night animal scurrying through the underbrush. A chuckle pursed his lips.

"The dark of night, Padre, is the time the devil collects his due. I don't need to tell you that. That's common knowledge to a man of the cloth, is it not?"

Carefully he laid the nearly dead weight on the lip of the highway. He took extra caution to make certain the priest's head didn't smash against the pavement.

"Lucky you, Padre, the pavement is still warm. Let us call it my way of giving comfort to the dying. No one wants to die alone in a cold, hard bed."

The man retightened his gloves and glanced up beyond the nearby peak of Mount Graham. The night sky was pregnant with a bounty of stars.

"It just doesn't get any more beautiful than this," he sighed. "Life is beautiful. And death...talk to me Father...is the Grim Reaper casting his shadow over you yet?"

Stepping down into the ditch, he grabbed the rocking chair and dragged it into the westbound lane. He triangulated with his hands to make certain the rocker was in the dead center of the lane.

"Fill in the blank for me, Padre. Death is...come on now. Death is...you know the answer. Death is...perfection," he sneered. "And...He is your next visitor."

Reaching under the unconscious priest's arms, he hoisted him into the chair. As the man stood back to survey his handiwork, he realized something was missing.

"Ah, yes. How silly of me."

His heart pitter-pattered with glee as he sprinted back through the underbrush to the station wagon. He reached under the seat.

"There you are. You little devil."

Dashing back through the arroyo, he emerged precisely where he had left his conquest.

"Here you go, Padre. You might want this where you're going."

He slipped the priest's personal Bible into his bluish fingers.

"I understand Saint Peter is partial to those who cough up an entrance fee."

The rites of Extreme Unction were administered ritualistically. When the sacrament was fully dispensed, he kissed the priest on the forehead. With a smile the blesser tipped the priest's head toward the heavens and hoarsely bellowed one final benediction.

"God, I know you are out there. I know you can hear me. Get ready. I am returning another sacrificial lamb to heaven's flock."

Having spoken his mind, the man trotted a half mile down the road where he had hidden his vehicle behind an abandoned gas station.

CHAPTER TWO

"It's a quarter to three,
There's no one in the place except you
and me."

The sweet strains of Frank Sinatra's voice were accompanied by the less than melodic warbling of a tone-deaf sheriff. Doreen, euphoric as never before in her thirty-three years, began to giggle infectiously. Swept away by the moment, Zeb Hanks belted it out with more false symphonic timbre than a dozen third-rate lounge acts.

"You'd never know it, but buddy I'm kind of a poet, and I've got a lot of things I'd like to say."

"Doreen, can you see the face of the man in the moon?"

"Of course."

"Can you hear what he's whispering?"

Doreen kissed her finger, pressed it against Zeb's lips and turned an ear toward the brightly shining orb.

"I hear that old man in the moon all right, but I can't quite make out the words."

Zeb ran his tongue over her finger. She felt weak in the knees.

"Doreen?"

"Yes, sugar dumplin'?

"That sweet old man in the moon is saying...will you marry me?"

The hushed quiet of the night became palpable. Chirping crickets paused. Creatures of the night froze in mid-step. Even the warm evening breeze calmed as it awaited a reply.

Doreen ran a caressing hand over her man's recently flattened stomach, stopping only when she reached the inside of his thigh. The tingle of pleasure it originally created suddenly turned to pain as she grabbed a pound of flesh.

"Ouch! Damn! What was that for?"

"I just wanted to make for certain you wasn't talkin' in your sleep...and that I wasn't dreamin'."

Doreen drew her flushed body tightly into her man's loving arms.

"Before you answer," said Zeb, "there is one important thing you have to think about."

"Is this the part where you prattle on 'bout the down side of bein' a sheriff's wife?"

"A cop's pay isn't so great. And the hours are terrible..."

"Do you think for half of one minute, what with the path I've beat through my life any of that would even matter?"

"It's not just..."

Before he could say another word, Doreen kissed him long and deep. She pulled back and stared into Zeb's moonlit eyes. Suddenly now didn't seem like the right time to tell her the Tucson Police Department had called today and made him an offer to return to his old position as a homicide detective. It sure as hell wasn't the time to let her know there were things he could never tell her about.

"Baby, I didn't fall in love with the badge. I fell in love with the man."

Her words rang true.

"It's just that I don't want you to worry every time the phone…"

As if on cue the ringer on Doreen's phone pierced the special feeling of the moment. Goosebumps involuntarily flared from every pore of her body as she grabbed the receiver.

"Hello."

"Doreen, this is Kate Steele. I'm so sorry to bother you, but I saw the sheriff's car parked in your driveway. I have to talk to him. It's very important."

"Don't think twice, hon, it's all right. I know it's business. Hang on one short sec."

"It's Kate," whispered Doreen, handing him the phone. "She says it's important."

"Deputy Steele, what's up?"

"We've got a situation."

"Go ahead."

"We've got a dead man, white male, undetermined age. We found his body three miles west of town on state route three, six, six, just beyond the Mount Graham Market."

"You know who it is?"

"Not yet. There was no ID. The body is mangled beyond recognition."

"Somebody dump him there?"

"No."

"Car go off the road?"

"No. Nothing quite that ordinary. It's rather strange. That's why I called you."

"Don't keep me in suspense, Deputy."

Sheriff Hanks cradled the phone between his shoulder and his ear. Using his finger, he made a writing motion against the palm of his hand. Doreen had already anticipated his need and was reaching into the nightstand for a pen.

"It looks like a suicide."

"Suicide?" asked the sheriff. "How do you figure?"

Heading into the kitchen to start a pot of coffee, Doreen reversed direction and returned to the bedroom upon hearing 'suicide'. She sat next to Zeb, placing an understanding hand on the leg she'd just pinched.

"Give me what you've got," said the sheriff, pointing to his pants and mouthing to Doreen, 'I need my clothes.'

"George Halvorson, owner of the Mount Graham Market, called it in about thirty minutes ago. He was rousted out of bed by a frantic trucker banging on his door. Mr. Halvorson described the driver as being in a state of shock. He said the trucker was unable to utter a complete thought. Even though George was in his pajamas, the trucker grabbed him by the arm and practically carried him to the spot where he'd just run over a man."

"Was the victim walking along the side of the road?"

"That's the odd part. Apparently the dead man had placed his rocking chair in the westbound lane in a depression just beyond where the road crests."

"Sweet mother of Jesus."

The mental image...a man sitting in a rocking chair...on a dark lonely stretch of road...in the middle of the night...flattened by an eighteen wheeler, made Zeb shudder.

"There's no way the driver barreling down the road at seventy miles an hour had any chance of seeing him, much less stopping. His truck hit the man head on. The man and the rocking chair were smashed to pieces. I'm sure the man died instantly."

"Thank God for small favors," mumbled the sheriff.

"Pardon me, Sheriff?"

"I was talking to myself. Go on."

"The driver panicked. He flipped his rig over into the ditch when he realized what happened."

"Have you talked with him?"

"He just keeps muttering. 'Man—rocking chair—middle of the road—I killed him'."

"Call Doc Yackley and let him know what's up. Better have him bring a sedative for the trucker. The poor son of a gun. Have Deputy Delbert get someone to tow the rig out of the ditch. I sure as hell don't want a bunch of gawkers hanging around there tomorrow morning causing more accidents. I'll be right there, shouldn't take me more than ten minutes."

"I haven't completely surveyed the entire scene yet," replied Deputy Steele. "I'll take care of things until you get here."

Zeb set the phone on the nightstand, tugged up his pants and turned to Doreen.

"Now that's about the damndest thing I ever heard."

"What is? Tell me what happened?" begged Doreen.

"We've just had a suicide."

"What's so crazy about that? There's been at least one every year since I moved to town," said Doreen. "Some people get depressed and see no way out of it but dyin'."

"It wasn't the suicide, Doe," said Zeb, slipping into his boots. "It was how it happened."

"Now dumplin', that ain't the kind of story you pull the reins in on halfway through. Tell your sugar what happened."

"It seems somebody took a rocking chair and placed it in the middle of the highway."

"Uh-oh."

"Then they sat themselves down and waited for an eighteen wheeler to come by and do the dirty work."

"Oh, dear Lord. Did Kate say who it was?"

"The body was mangled pretty badly. I guess we don't know just yet who it is."

"Is this the kind of thing you were warning me about? Middle of the night phone calls and all that?"

"I was trying to warn you death comes with the territory. I'm sorry to say it's part of the job."

"No need to be sorry about that," replied Doreen. "A man's got to do his job."

Zeb smiled and kissed her on the cheek.

"Why don't you try and get some rest," he suggested. "I'll come back when I see for myself what's happened."

"Good Gawd almighty, you know I couldn't go back to sleep after hearin' something like this. I might as well just go open up the café and get an early start at the day."

"Okay, then, I'll stop by the Town Talk after I have a look around out there."

"Zeb, honey bear, it's not like this every night, is it?"

"No," replied the sheriff. "It's usually pretty quiet."

Holding Doreen firmly in his arms, Zeb placed a parting kiss on her lips.

"Zeb, I got just an awful feeling flowin' through me right now. Baby, please be careful."

"Don't worry, Doe. I'll be careful. I always am."

The dull thud of Sheriff Zeb Hanks' boot heels on sidewalk cement and the distant hoot of a night owl broke the silence as dawn gave chase to what remained of the rapidly waning nighttime.

Opening the door of his patrol car, Zeb glanced toward the arched doorway where Doreen's mindful eye had been trailing his every step.

"You never did give me your final answer. What's it gonna be? Will you marry me?" shouted Zeb.

"Hush up now, sugar pie! You're going to wake the entire neighborhood. Then I'll have a heap of explainin' to do."

The sheriff turned his head toward a nosy neighbor's house as she flipped on an outside light and peeked through a curtain.

"Well, what's it gonna be? Yes or no?"

"Gee whiz, honey bun, give a girl a little time to let a big ol' question like that sink into her heart, would ya? It ain't everyday somebody offers up to change your life. Besides, it's good to keep a man wonderin'."

Zeb winked and waved.

"Fair enough. Take all the time you need between now and the next time you see my smiling face," he said.

Doreen watched Zeb's car turn the corner and pass beneath a lone street lamp lighting the intersection at the end of the block.

"I love you. When the time is right, I promise I'll tell you why I'm hesitant," she said softly. "But something is scarin' the bejesus outa me."

CHAPTER THREE

The first rays of the rising sun sparkled crisply against the golden rock faces of the highest elevations of Mount Graham. The purity of a new day dawning on the mountaintop bumped hard against the ghastly death image burning inside the sheriff's head. Who would do such a thing to himself? Why choose such a dramatic statement? He found himself agitated as he thought of how horribly indecent it was to have drawn a complete stranger into the personal act of suicide. He thought of the truck driver. His thought was simple, "Poor bastard will live with that the rest of his life."

The sheriff's thought was interrupted by what seemed a flash of sunlight glinting off his rearview mirror. He stiff-armed the steering wheel, instinctively straightening his posture. He squinted into the rearview mirror for a closer look. What he had incorrectly assumed to be reflected sunlight abruptly transformed into a pair of high beam headlights bearing down behind him at a dangerously fast pace. A split second later a candy apple red Cadillac Sedan Deville shot past him like a rocket. Dr. James Yackley was behind the wheel. Pressing down long and hard on the car horn, the old doctor stuck an arm out the window and gave the sheriff the thumbs up sign as he left the police cruiser in the dust.

"Jesus H. Christ, Doc, you're gonna get yourself killed if you don't slow down some," mumbled the sheriff as the whining Doppler effect of the car horn faded into the distance.

Two miles down the road Sheriff Hanks pulled into the graveled parking lot of the Mount Graham Market. Doc's flaming red Cadillac was parked obliquely, driver door flung wide open and the engine purring like a kitten. The sheriff reached in and switched off the ignition.

The market was a converted farmhouse from a decade's earlier cattle boom. It had definitely seen better days. The unpainted railing of the rotting wooden porch with half of its spindles missing was a perfect match for the toothless old timers who idled their days away jawboning about what might have been while resting their aging carcasses on equally run down chairs that lined the veranda. Death on the nearby road would give them fodder for half a year's worth of gossip.

Beneath the eerie glow of a dust-covered, neon bug zapper, George 'Grumpy' Halverson sucked down hard on the last quarter inch of a cigarette stub. Sitting nearby wrapped in an Indian blanket, a balding, middle-aged man with mutton chop sideburns rocked catatonically. Grumpy peered over the top of his glasses and pinched the remaining life out of the cigarette between a smoke-stained calloused thumb and bent finger.

He pointed the sheriff toward the wreck with a slight nod of the head.

At the edge of the parking lot, soft mauve and pink early morning hues painted the desert floor with splashes of color. The beauty of the desert landscape was harshly disrupted by a series of bright red flares placed near the tipped over semi-tractor trailer rig. Sheriff Hanks' deputy, Delbert Funke, surveyed the scene, hands on hips.

"We're over here, Sheriff."

Sheriff Hanks stepped over small splintered pieces of widely scattered rocking chair remains, making his way through the undergrowth.

"Watch where yer steppin', Sheriff".

The mangled wreck of a human body quickly came into the sheriff's scope of vision.

"The dead dude here is missin' a few parts. We don't want to be destroyin' no evidence."

Deputy Delbert crouched down, shining his flashlight under a small creosote bush.

"Looky here," he exclaimed. "It's an arm. Torn right off his body. I ain't never seen nothin' like it."

"Where's the rest of the body?" asked the sheriff.

Delbert pointed the flashlight beam behind a big rock about fifteen feet away.

"Scattered around. But most of it is right back there."

The dead man's remains were lying in a crumpled heap, stomach down. The head was twisted so far around on the body that it appeared like it had been placed backwards on his shoulders. A single open eyeball with the pupil dilated leaked a line of clear fluid.

"Looks like he's been cryin', don't it, Sheriff? But I don't suppose he felt any pain when the truck hit him. Do you?"

Sheriff Hanks glanced down at the tears on the dead man's cheek.

"If he did, it sure as hell didn't last too long." The sheriff directed the thin ray of the flashlight beam down the left side of the dead man's body. The stub of his arm rested in a pool of dark liquid.

Sheriff Hanks crouched. Something inside the ripped black shirt caught his attention. He reached in and pulled out a stiff white collar, like that of a cleric. Reaching forward, he dabbed a single finger into the thick and inky substance. He rubbed it in a circular motion between his thumb and first finger. A stain appeared on his roughened hand. Bringing his finger near his face, the sheriff took a shallow whiff. The unmistakable aromatic mixture of drying blood and death churned his stomach.

"Smells like skunked up late summer backwater, don't it, Sheriff?" said Delbert.

The sheriff pulled a handkerchief from his pocket and wiped away the greasy, sticky mixture.

"Jumpin' Jehovah!" cried Delbert.

Sheriff Hanks squinted in his deputy's direction.

"I think I'm standing on the dead man's hand."

"Take it easy, Deputy. His hand is over there, buried under the sand in that pool of blood," replied the sheriff.

"No, it ain't, Sheriff. It ain't buried 'neath nothin' 'cept my...foot."

"What are you talking about, Delbert?"

"Looky down here by my right foot. I just stepped on somethin'. I ain't certain but 'neath my boot it feels like a hand. It's givin' me the willies."

Sheriff Hanks shined the light near the deputy's boot heel.

"Lift up your foot, Delbert. I want to get a closer look."

The big deputy gingerly lifted his right foot and balanced all six feet six inches of his two hundred seventy-five pound body on a nervously unsteady left leg.

"No, it's not a hand," said the sheriff. "It's just a rock and some dead cactus spines."

"Whoa, whoa," yelled Delbert, tipping over and crashing into the underbrush. "Yeow, dang it all! Ouch! Ouch! Ouch!"

"You okay, Delbert?"

"I think so," cried the deputy reaching back to rub his head. "What the heck is this?"

"What's what?" asked the sheriff.

Delbert reached beneath a small bush that had cushioned his fall. Rubbing the back of his head and pulling cactus needles from his hair, Delbert handed a large book with a red leather cover to the sheriff.

"What the heck is a book doin' out here?" asked the deputy.

"It's a Bible," said the sheriff.

Sheriff Hanks instinctively opened the book. On the inside cover leaf was a handwritten inscription.

To Michael, my blessed son. Congratulations on this Holy Day, your ordination. I give you freely to God and the Sacred Order of St. Barnabus.
I am proud to call you Father McNamara.
Love Mother

Reading words of felicitation from a mother to her son gave the sheriff a shiver so powerful his shoulders jerked up involuntarily. But it was the flash of a second realization that nearly floored him.

"It's Father McNamara's Bible."

"No way!" exclaimed Delbert.

"From the inscription, it appears to be a gift from his mother on the day he became a priest."

"Geez. Now ain't that somethin'," added Delbert. "I mean that he had it with him when he croaked. But we still don't know it's him."

Sheriff Hanks and Deputy Delbert Funke stared blankly at the Bible, averting their eyes from the butchered body.

"Say, aren't Father McNamara and Doreen real close friends?"

"I suppose they know each other from the café," replied the sheriff.

"No, I mean…"

Delbert's statement was cut short by a shout from Deputy Steele. "Sheriff, I've found a billfold. The driver's license and credit cards belong to Father McNamara."

Zeb's heart sank as any hope of the body being someone other than the locally beloved Father McNamara faded quickly.

"Zeb."

Doc Yackley's thundering voice startled the men as he came barreling toward them.

"What the hell? What are you doing? Reading a book? Funny damn thing to be doing at a time like this."

"We ain't readin' it, Doc. We're just lookin' at it," answered Deputy Funke. "It's the personal Holy Bible of Father McNamara."

Sheriff Hanks tucked the Bible under his arm and pointed at the body of the priest. Doc Yackley knelt near the dead man.

"Damn knees of mine," grumbled Doc.

"You all right, Doc?" asked Delbert.

"Just my age and a touch of the 'tis. Nothing that being twenty years younger wouldn't cure," mumbled the doctor. "It's no damn concern of yours, that's for certain. Now who identified this man as Father McNamara? There's not enough left of his face to recognize him."

"The Bible is inscribed to him, and we got a wallet with his identification," said the sheriff.

"I'll tell you in ten seconds if it's him or not."

The old doctor unzipped the dead man's pants and pulled his underwear to the side revealing a red birthmark the size of a baseball. He tugged on a plastic tube implanted in the priest's body.

"Yup, we've got ourselves a dead priest all right. This is Father McNamara."

The doctor reached over and pulled the forearm out of the sand.

"You find his hand anywhere?" asked Doc. "He's seems to be missing it."

"Over here," said Deputy Steele. "I found it over here."

The doctor slowly brought himself to an upright position.

"Let me give you a hand, Doc," said Deputy Funke.

Doc Yackley brushed aside the offer.

"Is that some sort of pun, son?" asked Doc Yackley.

Delbert scratched his head as Sheriff Hanks chuckled.

"Just a little gallows humor, young man," added the doctor. "Don't worry your pretty little head about it."

"Don't worry, Doc. I won't. I never worry about nothin'," replied Deputy Delbert.

Deputy Delbert and Sheriff Hanks shined their

flashlights on the severed hand, an unnecessary act as the sun had risen well past dawn.

"It's a human hand all right. A left one."

Upon hearing Doc's explanation, Deputy Delbert glanced down at his palm, then the back of his own left hand. He repeated this gesture several times before finally extending his arm and holding his hand directly in his line of vision with the severed hand in the background.

"Yup, it's a southpaw all right. And there's a ring on the third finger."

Doc reached forward and carefully scraped particles of dirt and sand from the severed hand.

"With an inscription."

He reached into his coat pocket and removed a pair of bifocals.

Sheriff Hanks and his deputy leaned forward as Doc brought his face to within inches of the excised hand.

"Let's see here. It's written in Latin."

"You read Latin, Doc?"

The savvy old country doctor winked at the sheriff.

"I suppose I'm going to have to if I want to know what this damn ring says."

"No foolin', Doc. You can do that? You can just look at another language and read it?" asked Delbert. "Now that's really something."

"Helps being a doctor. Lot of our secret stuff is written in Latin and Greek."

"Oh, I see," replied the deputy. "That makes a

heap a sense."

"Now let me see. It says here...Ordinis Sancti Barnabae Vat Astronomicis Observatorium, Basilicam Sancti Petri...I would say that translates roughly as Order of St. Barnabas, Vatican Astronomical Observatory, Basilica St. Peter. There's a picture here, too."

Doc Yackley squinted, moving his head a bit closer to the ring. After a moment he took off his glasses and cleaned them on his untucked and rumpled shirt.

"There, that oughta make seein' things a bit smoother."

Returning the cheaters to his face, Doc scrunched his cheekbones back and forth, allowing his glasses to slip down to the tip of his nose.

"Yes, that's better. It's a picture of a building. Hmm. It looks sort of like an old- fashioned tower up on a hillside in front of a church. Likely the Vatican Astronomical Observatory."

The rising sun now fully illuminated the eastern slopes of Mount Graham. Coming from the direction of town, Sheriff Hanks eyed the hearse from Shepner's Funeral Home making its way down Route 366 toward the death scene.

"Never a welcome sight, is it?" said Doc Yackley, observing the sheriff honing in on the death wagon.

"Nope, never is."

"Doesn't seem to be much of a need for a full

blown autopsy. I'll take some blood and tissue and give it a routine once over. Is that okay with you?" inquired the doctor. "I mean with the birthmark and the colostomy bag, odds are one in a million it could be anyone else."

"Colostomy bag?" asked Sheriff Hanks.

"Father McNamara had stage four colo-rectal cancer. He was in the end stages of life. He had a month at best. He was headed for hospice care real soon."

Zeb and Doc exchanged a glance that spoke to the hidden fear all people have. What would they do under the same circumstances?

"Out of respect for his position at the church, I imagine it will be just fine if we let Shepner's do their business and leave it at that," replied the sheriff. "I think the cause of death is pretty damn obvious. No sense making it any worse for his congregation by delaying the funeral."

"I guess that settles it. I'll take some blood samples and get my medical report to you later this morning. The official cause of death looks like it's going to be suicide unless that trucker over there's got a different story."

Doc Yackley pointed to the porch where the distraught trucker continued his manic rocking.

"Why don't you come along and we'll have a little chat with him? That way he can say it once and hopefully I can be done with it, legally anyhow," suggested Zeb.

"Let's get crackin' then," said Doc. "I'd like to

grab a bite of breakfast before I start my rounds at the hospital. Better have Delbert snoop around a little more before they load up the body. Father McNamara is missing both his shoes and his left foot was severed just above the ankle. And don't forget the hand. Make sure Shepner's gets it."

"Oh, crap," moaned Delbert, "more missin' body parts. Gad, I hate touchin' that kinda stuff. It gives me the creeps."

Deputy Delbert Funke half-heartedly began to look around for the shoes and missing foot of the priest as the hearse driver and his assistant came scrambling up the small knoll with a stretcher.

Sheriff Hanks and Doc Yackley slowly made their way toward the Mount Graham Market and the traumatized trucker.

"I already gave him a light sedative, ten milligrams of Valium, to calm his nerves. Poor son of a bitch was pretty shook. He should be okay to talk, unless the Valium fogs him out."

Grumpy Halvorson and the truck driver sat on the porch chairs sipping coffee. The trucker stared off into space, mumbling incoherently as he swayed rhythmically to some unheard beat.

"Doc, that shot you gave him made him a little goofy, so I gave him a little good morning cactus juice to straighten him up. I figured the sheriff would want to have a word or two with him. Fella' says his name is Billy Joe Thomas. Operates his rig out of Yuma."

"Thanks, George."

"Billy Joe, my name is Sheriff Hanks. You already met Doc Yackley."

"Sheriff Hanks, pleased to meet you. Doctor Yackley, whatever you gave me sure helped to calm down my jits."

"I'm glad it helped," smiled Doc. "It's been a rough day for you."

"You can say that again."

A wave of pity came over Zeb. He knew that killing a man, even accidentally, was a shocking burden that would lessen with time but never go away.

"I need to go over a few things with you," began the sheriff, "for my official report. You feel like talking?"

"I suppose. It's gotta be done sooner or later."

At the mention of the accident, the trucker increased his nervous swaying.

"Why don't you start by telling me what happened," said the sheriff.

"I wasn't speeding. And I wasn't over on my driving time. You can go right ahead and check my log. I swear I wasn't even tired."

"Uh-huh. Go ahead and tell me what happened," said the sheriff.

"There's not much to say really. It was so weird. It was almost like it happened in slow motion. At first I thought I was seeing things. You would have too. I mean it isn't every day you see something like that."

"What did you see?"

"I was heading west on three-six-six, doing about sixty three, sixty four miles per hour, not so fast that I didn't have complete control of my rig. Anyway back up that way…"

The trucker weakly lifted a shaky arm and pointed down the road.

"…where the highway begins to rise up a coyote scampered across the road. I watched him skulk off into the desert. I remember thinking the little critter looked mighty scruffy. When I looked back up, right over there where the road peaks and then goes down into that little depression, I caught sight of something out of the corner of my eye. At first I couldn't believe I was seeing what I was seeing. It didn't make any sense in my mind. Right there in the middle of the road was a man dressed all in black."

The trucker became mute as he stared at the accident site.

"Pardon me, Sheriff, but I was seeing it all over again. The man was dressed all in black except for a white collar around his neck. I think it was a white collar. Time slowed down. It was crazy. He was sitting in a rocking chair, smack dab in the middle of the road. Can you believe it? How does something like that come to be?"

The trucker sipped from the coffee cup cradled gingerly in his unsteady hands. His head tipped forward after taking a drink. He began to weep softly.

"There was nothing I could do. There wasn't

time to swerve. I tried to turn out of the way, but it was too late." The driver paused as tears welled in his eyes and his voice became a choked rasp. "I hit him with my right front bumper. He flipped right out of the chair and came flying through the air. His face smashed against my windshield. The whole thing seemed like it was happening to somebody else. It was like I was watching a movie."

Grumpy Halvorson whispered under his breath. "Jesus."

"Just take your time," said the sheriff. "I know it's difficult."

"Thank you," said the trembling man. "Like I said, the whole darn thing happened in slow motion. That's how come I can remember it so good. When he came crashing in against my windshield, he just stopped there, pressed up against the window. I didn't want to look because his face was all mangled and twisted. But I couldn't help it. I had to look."

The sheriff, Doc and Grumpy remained quiet as the man took a moment to regain his composure.

"His arm was crunched up under his chest. He was holding onto a book. I could even read the words on the cover. HOLY BIBLE. That's right. He was holding a Bible in his hands. What with the Bible and the black clothes and his collar, I knew he was a priest. It's got to be some kind of an omen."

The trucker's face carried the fearful, forlorn

grimace of a condemned man.

"Take it easy there, Billy Joe. No one here is passing any kind of judgment on you."

Sheriff Hanks' reassurance seemed to ease the trucker's angst.

"I'm a good man. I don't go to church regularly. I used to be a good Catholic, but I gave it up to become a real Christian. I know I'm going right to hell for killing a priest. No two ways about it. Everybody knows you go straight to hell when you kill a priest. It's one of God's most basic laws."

"It wasn't your fault," interrupted the doctor. "Try not to torture your mind with it."

"It's too late for that. I'm a condemned man."

"Just try and take it easy," said Doc.

"I can't take it easy because it's what happened next that really freaked me out and made me realize it was the work of the devil."

"What was that?" asked Sheriff Hanks.

"The priest kept a hold on that Bible like he couldn't let go even in death. His face was up against the glass right there in front of my eyes for what seemed like an eternity. And the Good Book, there it was, still clenched in his grip. I think I hit a pot hole then or slammed on my air breaks or something and whammo, he goes flyin' off the windshield...and then..."

Some unspoken thought caused the man to begin sobbing hysterically. Grumpy handed him some Kleenex.

"Take your time," the sheriff counseled.

"...I got so scared that I put Old Betsy in the ditch."

"Old Betsy?"

"My rig is my Betsy. I named her after my grandmother."

"I think we ought to leave him be for a while."

Sheriff Hanks knew by the tone of Doc's voice that this suggestion fell under the category of doctor's orders.

"Why don't you get a room at the Trails West Motel? Call your family. Get some rest. My deputy will give you a ride over there."

"Thank you," muttered the trucker, holding his head in his hands.

"I'll stop by later after you've had some time to rest. If you think of anything else, tell me then or give me a call."

Sheriff Hanks handed the man his business card.

"I didn't mean to kill him, Sheriff. It was an accident, honest."

"Tell him, Zeb. So his mind can rest," said Doc Yackley.

"Tell me what?" asked the bewildered trucker.

"If what you're telling me is the truth, and at this time I don't have any reason to believe you aren't, his death wasn't your fault."

"*What?* Of course it was my fault. I killed him."

Sheriff Hanks placed his hand on the confused trucker's shoulder.

"I'm fairly certain we're going to rule Father McNamara's death a suicide."

"A priest can't commit suicide," said the trucker. "It's a mortal sin."

"I'm afraid this one did," said the sheriff.

"Does the priest have any family nearby?"

"A lot of friends, a good lot of parishioners, but not any relatives that I know of," said the sheriff.

On the road back to town, a quarter mile or so from the death scene, early rays of sunshine glinted off something just to the side of the road. It took Sheriff Hanks about five seconds to recognize the abandoned station wagon that belonged to the dead priest. He examined it briefly and called for a tow truck to haul it to Zip's garage where it could be looked over more closely.

CHAPTER FOUR

"Good afternoon, Jake."

"Helen, you're looking as lovely as always. You still hitchin' your pony to the same old wagon?"

Helen Nazelrod, secretary extraordinaire to Sheriff Hanks, blushed needlessly at her old boss, former sheriff Jake Dablo's kidding compliment.

"Of course I am, Jake, you know that," she said. "Thirty one years and still going strong."

"Well if things ever change, be sure and let me know."

"You'll be the first to know, I assure you," said Helen. "Other than your usual nonsense what brings you around the sheriff's office? You're not looking for your old job back, are you?"

"No, nothing like that," laughed Jake. "I've got my hands full working with the county these days. Between the planning commission and shaking dice over at the Town Talk, I hardly have any time left over for myself."

"Well, I'm sure we could always find a position for you around here if you're ever looking for real work."

"Thanks, Helen. I'll keep it in mind. Is the sheriff in?"

"He's pretending to do some paperwork that I already did for him," said Helen. "Go right in. I doubt you'll interrupt his concentration."

Helen and Jake exchanged winks as the former lawman strolled into the familiar surroundings of what had been his office a decade earlier.

"Top of the morning, Jake."

"Zeb, you look a little boxed in behind that desk. Buried in paperwork, eh?"

"Up to my eye teeth in it. Have a seat. I can use the break."

Zeb pointed to a timeworn chair directly across from his desk.

"You know I always liked this old thing, but I don't think I ever had an opportunity to sit in it back when I was sheriff."

Jake patted the soft leather of the oversized chair as he made himself comfortable.

"Shouldn't you be out fishing or something on a fine day like this?" asked Zeb.

"People go fishing to escape," said Jake. "I don't have much I need to get away from these days."

"So what brings you around then? Is this a social visit or is something on your mind?"

"That's a good way of putting it. I guess you could say that something is sort of on my mind. It's something I think you ought to know about. It's probably nothing, but, then again, it might be something."

"Spit it out, Jake. I'm all ears." Jake smiled at the self-deprecation. Zeb did have ears that stuck out a bit more than most.

"Like I said, maybe it's something and maybe

it's not. It's just one of those things I have a funny feeling about. Nothing I can pinpoint exactly."

"It's not like you to beat around the bush, Jake. What's this got to do with?"

"The county planning commission," replied Jake.

"How do you like being a bureaucrat, anyway?"

"The job isn't so bad. It keeps me up on what's happening in the area, but it does seem to be taking a lot more of my time than I thought it might."

"That right there is a reason to go fishing."

Jake's failure to laugh at his little joke told Zeb something serious was on his former mentor's mind. Zeb put his paperwork down, leaned back in his chair and folded his arms across his chest.

"So what's up? State rules and regs getting to you? Or is old man Farrell driving you nuts?" asked Zeb.

"Farrell has his ways. He's a bit on the secretive side. He operates a bit differently than most other folks do."

"A bit underhanded from what I hear," said Zeb. "Even maybe what you might call shifty?"

"Crafty might be a better word for it," said Jake.

The men exchanged knowing smiles through poker faces.

"So what's up?" asked the sheriff.

"The planning commission has a meeting tonight."

"Nothing unusual about that, is there?"

"Normally I would say, no, there isn't. But this is a different situation."

"How so?"

"Our scheduled meeting is on the first Thursday of every month."

"Just like clockwork," said Zeb. "Like the good public servants you are."

Around Graham County people made no bones about their belief that the job of the planning commissioner was little more than a rubber stamp for the county, or worse, for businesses that profited at the expense of the citizens or the environment. The negative attitude mostly had to do with real estate developers who had nothing but a quick buck on their mind. Locals had more than once seen scam artists buy up huge chunks of worthless desert land and resell it in parcels to unsuspecting dupes right under the noses of the commission. Jake had volunteered for the commission knowing it would be an uphill battle to make it a dignified organization.

"You said it. Like clockwork, always like clockwork," said Jake. "That's why this seems odd to me. Tonight's the fourth Tuesday of the month. John Farrell called me last night to tell me about it."

"I guess he's got the right to call a meeting if he wants to. After all, he is the chairman."

"Yes, he is, and that's all well and good. But when he called, he specifically asked me not to mention the meeting to anyone."

"Has he ever asked you to keep mum before?"

"Never."

"Did he say why he wanted to meet tonight?"

"No, he didn't, and the whole damn thing smells rotten. As you know, the county planning commission meetings are open to everyone. Our charter says the general public has to be notified of all meetings, unless it's an emergency."

"There's your answer. It's an emergency meeting."

"I asked him about that. It's not."

"Hmm. Did you ask him why he didn't want you telling anyone?"

"As a matter of fact I did."

"What did he say?"

"He was as vague as a politician during election season. He claimed the meeting had to do with something that was going to be real good for the county. He said if the commission wasted any time the so called 'good thing' might not happen."

"Did he tell you what this 'good thing' was?"

"He wouldn't say. He just kept taking the subject somewhere else whenever I brought it up."

"What are you telling me all this for, Jake? What do you want me to do? It isn't like he's committed some sort of crime. Everyone knows he's a sneaky little varmint. I'm certain if anybody asks about the meeting, Farrell will just say it was an emergency. You know as well as I do he knows the ropes and exactly what he can get away with."

"You're not telling me anything I don't already know, Zeb."

"Then what do you figure I can do?"

"I don't *figure* you can do anything, other than attend the meeting to witness the groundwork for whatever the hell is going to go down."

"You can get anybody to do that. Why do you need me?" asked Zeb.

"I smell a rat. Call it an ex-lawman's uneasy hunch. I suspect somebody is trying to pull a fast one. I need you because I'll need somebody with a whole lot of respect in the county to back me, in case I'm right."

"You need *me* to cover *your* ass at a county commission meeting? When I was your deputy, you wouldn't call for back up unless...come to think of it you never called for backup," laughed Zeb. "Jake, you aren't as tough as you used to be."

"Zeb, you know exactly what I'm talking about. If somebody is up to some sort of shenanigans, I want a second set of eyes and ears backing me up. I need a respected member of the community to bear witness."

"Jake, you wouldn't be here asking me to cover your ass unless you suspected a whole lot more than you're letting on. Let's have it."

"You were a good deputy under me, Zeb. And I'm beginning to believe you're an even better sheriff."

Ex-sheriff Jake Dablo looked beyond Sheriff Hanks toward the partially opened office door. Outside the door, Helen Nazelrod, as usual, was all ears. Zeb got up and closed the door. Helen cleared her throat and harumphed loudly.

"Some things never change, do they?"

"Go on now, Jake, let me have it. What do you really think is going on?" asked Zeb.

"Eskadi Black Robes stopped by the other day to talk. It was sort of off the record, sort of in his official capacity as tribal chairman. This was shortly after your deputy, Kate Steele, delivered a foreclosure notice to Beulah Trees last week out on the San Carlos Reservation."

"Sure, I remember."

"Beulah's nearly a century old. Since she can't see so good even with her glasses, she had one of her great-grandchildren give her a ride over to the tribal council building to have someone read it to her and explain what it all meant.

"I've heard she's a feisty old gal," said Zeb.

"You can say that again," said Jake. "She marched right into Eskadi's office, laid the notice down on his desk and told him she wanted to know what it meant. I heard she plopped down in a chair and told him she wasn't moving until he explained it to her in a way she could understand."

"Eskadi's been doing a decent job as tribal chairman. He keeps an eye on those that can't look after themselves. He's a touch on the radical side, but with all those educational programs he is starting out on the San Carlos, I can put his politics aside for the most part. He's a good man all right. I believe I can trust him."

"Anyway, he read the foreclosure notice over once. Then he read it out loud from start to finish for Beulah. According to Eskadi, all the legal mumbo-jumbo nearly put old Beulah to sleep."

The thought of Eskadi reading the elderly Beulah Trees to sleep brought a smile to the sheriff's face.

"When he was done, he explained to Beulah it all appeared legal enough. He told her maybe the tribe could try and get a tax abatement for her being that she had never gotten a proper tax assessment, according to her recollection anyway. But old Mrs. Trees wouldn't have any part of it. She told Eskadi no one had any right to own a piece of the Sacred Mountain, including her."

"So what's any of this got to do with the price of peanuts in Poland, or for that matter John Farrell calling a special planning commission meeting you want me to witness?"

"Just hang on for a minute. Let me finish my story and you'll find out. Once Eskadi made a copy of the foreclosure notice, he gave Beulah a ride back home. On the road back to her house they got to talking about the old ways, traditional ways. You know how Eskadi is interested in that sort of thing."

"Do I ever. He's always trying to teach me

about how things were and how they ought to be that way again. He believes the world won't ever be in harmony until the Apaches get back what is rightfully theirs."

"Beulah started wagging on about the old days. She told Eskadi when it got hot during the summer, practically everyone from the entire San Carlos Reservation would go up to the top of Mount Graham because it was so much cooler. When she was little, whole villages would go up there for two or three months at a time. She told Eskadi about lying under the stars and how the old wise ones would tell the Apache creation story."

"Knowing Eskadi, I bet that sort of reminiscence touched a soft spot in his heart," said Zeb. "And five will get you ten that with your interest in mythology and the stars, not to mention storytelling, I'll just bet you didn't hesitate to sit back and suck it all in."

"It touched me all right, but that's beside the point. When Eskadi got back to his office, he read Beulah's letter again. He told me it seemed just fine from a legal point of view, but something made him very curious."

"What lit the fire under his ass this time?"

"A great big law firm from up in Phoenix was handling the case."

"What's that got to do with anything?"

"It struck Eskadi as odd that a large law firm from Phoenix would be handling a foreclosure on such a small property in rural Arizona. He called it a one sided shootin' match. A big city law firm putting the hammer down hard on a poor, little, defenseless, century-old Indian woman reminded him of how it took damn near the entire US Cavalry to capture Geronimo."

"Now that sounds like Eskadi."

"So he decided to do a little investigation of his own. He started out by giving the law firm a call."

"I'm telling you when Eskadi Black Robes gets a burr under his saddle, he doesn't rest until he finds the source of the irritation. I've said it to his face so I can say it to you. That education he got out there in California is as much of a curse on him as it is a blessing."

"I know it, but you must admit that he has mellowed a bit"

"Thank the lord for small favors," replied Zeb.

"When you think about it, what chance does a hundred-year-old Apache woman stand against a big corporate attorney? You can't hardly call that an even shake of the dice."

"You'll get no argument from me. So what did Eskadi find out when he called the law firm?"

"Eskadi's always been a bit on the cagey side. I don't mind saying that a part of me admires his tenacity," said Jake. "But, in this case, his tricky ways may have just landed his nose into a much larger can of worms."

"Go on now, Jake, you've got my curiosity roused."

"The law firm specializes in large real estate deals, development of housing and business properties. From b.s.'ing with somebody, Eskadi discovered the law firm has been handling a significant number of land deals out on Mount Graham."

"Did Eskadi find out why?"

"Not directly from the law firm itself, but he finagled information from John Farrell's secretary, Darla Thompson, over at the real estate office."

"You're jumping ahead of yourself, Jake. How is Farrell's secretary involved with all this?"

"Sorry. When Eskadi got done talking to those folks up in Phoenix at the law firm, he decided to call Rodeo Real Estate to see if they knew anything about land sales on Mount Graham. He told me he chose Farrell's office because he had the largest ad in the phone book. Eskadi proceeded to butter up the secretary. She sang like a caged canary. Apparently in the last three years Farrell has sold thirty or forty parcels of land, mostly small ones, a couple of acres here, three or four there, up on the mountain."

"Holy cow, that's a lot of deals. I haven't heard anything about it."

"Neither had anyone else around town, except Farrell and his secretary."

Outside of the sheriff's door the wooden floor squeaked. Both men knew Helen Nazelrod's modus operandi included finding a reason to press her ear against the keyhole. Crafty but caught, Helen knocked on the door.

"Yes, Helen," shouted the men in unison.

"Coffee?"

Helen burst through the door acting as innocently as a guilty person could.

"Can I bring you men some coffee? A sweet roll maybe?"

The men nodded in the affirmative. One minute later Helen returned with the coffee and rolls. She set them down in front of the men and turned to leave without saying a word. As she slowly closed the creaking door, she gave it a little extra tug, sending a reverberation throughout the office.

"Better get Helen a couple of blueberry muffins next time you're over at the Town Talk, or she's likely to stay huffy with you for a day or two."

"I know the routine. For what it's worth, Jake, you are right when you say some things around here never do change. After this much time of working with Helen I think I'm onto something."

"You think you've got Helen figured out?"

"Yup," replied Zeb proudly. "Blood sugar."

"Blood sugar?"

"You know how she gets a little ornery and the slightest thing you do can get her undies in a bunch?"

"You mean like not letting her snoop in on private conversations?"

"You saw it for years when you were sheriff. What's the one thing that always puts her back into your good graces?"

"A blueberry muffin."

"Exactly. Her blood sugar gets a little low, she eats a muffin and she's fine."

"Is this something Doc cooked up?"

"Nope, I read about it in the *Inquirer*. You should pick it up some time. It's loaded with great information."

"I'll keep that in mind."

"Now what was it you were telling me about Eskadi and the Phoenix real estate agency? Who the hell is interested in that much land up there anyway?"

"I'm glad your inquiring mind wants to know. Eskadi claims all of the purchased land was put into a land trust for a foreign corporation."

"What would a foreign corporation want with land on top of Mount Graham?" asked Zeb.

"Beats the heck out of me, but I think the planning commission meeting tonight has something to do with it. That is why I want you there."

"What do you suspect is *really* going on?"

"I don't really know, but, like I said, the whole damn thing has been shrouded in so much secrecy, it stinks. I suspect Farrell's involved in some kind of mischief. He's sold all that property up there and not crowed about it to anyone. That's damn strange for a man who never misses an opportunity to brag about what a great salesman he is."

Sheriff Hanks knew Jake Dablo wasn't prone to exaggeration or paranoia. But somehow his hunch, which lacked any cold hard facts, seemed a little far-fetched. Jake Dablo had given up the booze and straightened his life out since he had lost nearly everything after the brutal murder of his granddaughter. Nevertheless, all those years of hard living and carrying around a heart full of hate may have taken a toll on his reason. On the other hand, during the years they worked side by side, Jake was more rational and logical than anyone Zeb had ever known. It did seem odd that a bunch of foreigners were buying land on Mount Graham through a law firm in Phoenix. If it did turn out to be a swindle, then it would be sheriff business. Zeb thought about it. When truth crisscrossed the bottom line, the least he owed Jake was a couple of measly hours at a commission meeting. What harm could it do?

"What the hell. I'll see you at the meeting."

"Thanks, Zeb. Hopefully, it won't turn out to be anything."

Jake pushed his way up out of the leather chair. He reached over to shake the hand of his longtime friend.

"Tonight, around seven?"

"Seven o'clock sharp it is."

Sheriff Hanks plopped down in his chair and started in on some overdue paperwork. The tasks at hand didn't prevent his mind from wandering to Doreen Nightingale. How long was it going to be before she gave him an answer to his marriage proposal? A day, a month, a year? Though the anticipation was uncomfortable, he knew he would be a darned fool to try and influence her decision by forcing a timetable. He would remain patient.

Zeb placed his pen on top of his work. He imagined Doreen as a beautiful bride wearing a white wedding gown, floating down the aisle of Saint Barnabas Catholic Church. He chuckled as he thought of himself looking like a penguin in a rented tuxedo, but it would please her. Standing at the altar of Saint Barnabas Catholic Church, they would be married by a Catholic priest.

The lightness of the moment became gray and dim with the thought of Father Michael McNamara. It had been a month since Father McNamara's death. Doreen's ever fervent insistence that it was something other than suicide was creating a rift between them. Her explanation, however, was understandable. She had been seeing Father McNamara about reconstituting her faith. In the process they had talked about mortal sins. One of the mortal sins was suicide. Father McNamara and Doreen had deep and lengthy conversations on the subject. Why they talked so much about suicide was not something Doreen had yet shared with Zeb.

Zeb tapped his pen nervously atop the pile of paperwork. The strange death of Father McNamara weighed heavily on his mind. He could not shake the image of the priest sitting in his rocking chair, in the middle of a highway, patiently waiting for the Angel of Death to greet him in the form of an eighteen-wheeled semi-truck. How strange that Father McNamara should have been struck so forcefully, flung through the air, body crushed against the windshield and yet his Bible remained clutched tightly in his hand. Lost in thought, Zeb didn't hear Helen creep into this office.

"Sheriff, Jake Dablo just asked me to give you a message."

Helen Nazelrod's voice was a welcome break from the ugliness he had conjured up in his mind.

"Yes? What did he want?"

"He told me to tell you the county planning commission meeting was canceled."

"Did he say why?"

"No. He just told me to tell you the meeting was canceled."

"Thanks."

Sheriff Hanks glanced at his wristwatch and reached for the phone.

"Town Talk, home of the one and only red hot Tex-Mex burger. Come on down, immediate seating available."

"Doreen, this is Zeb."

"Hey, sunshine. Did you call lil' ol' me just to brighten up my day?"

"Maybe. How'd you like to go for a little spin around sunset?"

"Well, honeybunch, I got a business to run, but I suppose I can sneak out for the likes of you. That is, if I can get Maxine to close up for me."

"I'll pick you up around quarter to eight. Can you be ready by then?"

"For a handsome fella' like you, a gal like me can get herself ready in two shakes of a lamb's tail. Just out of curiosity, where are you planning on takin' me?"

"I thought you might like to watch the sunset from up top of Mount Graham."

"You are the romantic one, aren't you, sweetums?"

He didn't mention the trip was mostly business.

CHAPTER FIVE

Zeb's heart quickened slightly as he turned down Main Street. Standing on the sidewalk, primping her hair in the diner window, stood the woman his heart had fallen for.

Eyeing the superimposed reflection of Zeb's truck in the glass, Doreen spun around and waved happily. Zeb returned the gesture as he parked the Dodge Ram pickup in front of the Town Talk.

"Hello there, snooky-ookums! How shines the love-light of my life?"

Doreen's dramatic public display of affection always managed to embarrass him but not today. He smiled as Doreen bounded down from the curb. Sticking her head through the driver's window, she gave the startled sheriff a big smooch on the lips.

"Don't act so surprised when your sugar gives you a little sugar," admonished Doreen.

A goofy grin spread across Zeb's face as Doreen turned and sashayed in front of the car. In a moment of levity he wiggled his fingers and winked at her from behind the wheel of his truck. His greeting was met with a tossed kiss. He put his fingertips to his lips and returned the lovebird gesture. Watching all of this from a window booth in the Town Talk was a coffee klatch comprised of some of the town's most respected senior women. In unison, they returned his flying kiss with one of their own. The sheriff's face flushed with embarrassment. Doreen slid in across the front seat, snuggled up next to her man and planted a second soft, sweet kiss on his lips.

"What's going on here?" asked the sheriff suspiciously. "I feel like I'm on public display."

"Those lil' ol' sweeties in there." Doreen nodded to the window. "All four of 'em are widows. They were in the middle of givin' me some advice when I saw your truck comin' down the street. Them gals and me got an understandin' of each other."

"And exactly what sort of advice were you taking from those gals?"

"Shucks, Zeb, they know we're datin' so I told them you was takin' me up on Mount Graham for a sunset serenade."

"Is that right?"

"Sure enough is. When I told 'em what a romantic fella you was, they started to cackle and haw. The excitement spread around the table like wild brush fire. Next thing I knew, they were teasin' me like there was no tomorrow, especially the Widow Kemper."

"She's been married three times and all of her husbands died in bed," said Zeb. "I've heard plenty of stories about her."

"She bet me a plug nickel I couldn't steal a pair of kisses from you inside of thirty seconds of layin' my eyes on ya'."

"I think you won the bet."

"I surely did and you know what?"

"What?"

"I can double my winnings if you throw your arms around me and give me a coupla more wet ones."

"Oh, what the heck," said Zeb. "Let's give them their money's worth."

Zeb wrapped Doreen up in his arms and planted a kiss on her lips.

"Hooeee! I do like that kinda monkey business."

In the window the four widow women clapped, laughed and pointed toward the kissing couple. Doreen waved to the happy women. Zeb backed the truck into the street and slipped a cassette tape of Doreen's favorite music into the deck. She leaned over, kissed him on the earlobe and mussed his thick hair as strains of Sara Vaughan's *Vanity* aired sweetly through the sound system.

"You've never taken me up the mountain for sunset before," said Doreen. "What's the occasion?"

"I haven't done it myself, since I was a kid anyway. I figured that you might like it."

"So, you were thinkin' of me, weren't you, dumplin'?"

"As a matter of fact I was. For some reason you came into my mind right out of the blue today. I was frustrated and tired and feeling overworked..."

"Well pop my balloon and watch me fizzle. Ain't that a fine bunch of reasons to think of a gal?"

"Give a guy a chance to finish, will you?"

"I'm just joshin'. You know that."

"I know, Doe. Anyway, what I was trying to say was, well I was having a bad day. A rotten day that was headed further south. But the one thing that eased my mind was thinking about you."

Doreen rubbed the smooth back of her hand lovingly against the stubby growth of facial hair sprouting on Zeb's cheek. His blue eyes sparkled against the waning sun as he turned to her and smiled sweetly.

"Then I thought of how peaceful it is up top the Mount and, shucks, I put one and one together and figured this was the perfect time to show you one of my all-time favorite spots."

Doreen rested her head softly on Zeb's broad shoulder and hummed along with Sara Vaughn. Near the intersection of Route 366 and Highway 191 a decansos replete with fresh flowers, statues of the Blessed Mother, Jesus Christ and Saint Barnabus along with dozens of lighted candles kept tribute to the memory of Father McNamara. Doreen nuzzled a little closer, drawing Zeb's arm to her breast. Her fluttering eyes met his longing gaze.

"You know something, Zeb?"

"What, Doe?"

"I think I might just be fallin' deep enough in love with you to take you up on your offer."

"Does that mean you'll marry me?"

"Yes, Zeb, I will marry you. When I..."

Doreen hesitated. Zeb felt the hair on the back of his neck stand up as Sara Vaughan sang in the background...

> *I never even glance when offered new romance*
> *I can't because I'm yours...and yours alone.*

"When I straighten out something in my head that needs to get straightened out."

Zeb felt his heart sink. He paused for a second or two and then asked, "Can you tell me what needs to be straightened out?"

"Not just yet. It's what I was talkin' with Father McNamara about. Let's not talk about it anymore. At least not right now. I don't want to spoil a perfect moment."

"Okay," replied Zeb. "As long as I know that you won't wait forever to tell me what it is that needs straightening out."

"I won't," said Doreen. "I will tell you when the time is right. For now, let's just love each other."

Zeb pulled the truck off the road at Riggs Lake. The pink underbelly of low-hanging clouds on the western horizon paid homage to the waning moments of the day. Shades of early evening sneaked like a thief in the night across the east face of Mount Graham. Years had passed since he had last driven up the winding, ever changing mountain road at dusk. The powerful and ultimate beauty attached to witnessing daylight quietly slip away into night reminded him once more of the sanctity of the mountain.

"It's precious here," whispered Doreen. "Maybe the most beautiful spot I've ever seen."

"It's my favorite place anywhere on earth at this time of day. It's been too long since I've been here."

"Zeb, honey, I'm so glad you're sharin' it with me."

Tender tears welled in Doreen's eyes as she slipped her arms around Zeb. Pressing her lips against his cheek, teardrops gently fell from her eyes.

"What's this?" asked Zeb. "Did I say the wrong thing?"

"No nothin' like that. I feel good, that's all."

Zeb shook his head and smiled.

"If I live to be a hundred years old, I swear I will never understand women."

"You don't have to, honey bunch. And it's probably best you don't."

"Come on," said Zeb. "I have something I want to show you."

"Just a second," said Doreen. "Can I say somethin' first? I got somethin' just weighin' heavy on my chest that needs sayin'."

"Of course."

"Promise me what I say won't hurt your feelings."

"What?" asked Zeb.

"Go on, promise."

He knew when Doreen wanted his vow stated aloud. He gave it to her.

"Okay Doe, what is it?"

"I know you're the best damn sheriff in the state and that nothin' gets by the likes of you..."

"That statement sounds like it has a 'but' attached to it."

"It does. But, I know in my heart that Father McNamara didn't commit suicide. I just know somethin' else happened. I can't say what exactly, but I know he wouldn't kill himself. He wasn't like that. I know it for certain as I know I love you."

"Honey, the state came down and investigated. So did some people from the Catholic Church. Everyone has come to the same conclusion. Doc Yackley is waiting on a couple of post mortem blood tests, but I doubt they'll show anything. I'm sorry. I wish I could make the pain of his death disappear, but I can't. You're just going to have to be patient and let time do the healing. Okay?"

Doreen pouted with her lower lip and nodded. She shook her head side to side. She looked him directly in the eyes.

"One day you will know, Zeb Hanks, one day you will know how I am so certain."

Zeb had the sudden realization that there were deep and dark secrets hidden inside the woman he loved. He loved her. He could wait to find out exactly what they were.

CHAPTER SIX

Zeb stepped out and held the car door open for Doreen. Opening the trunk of his car, Zeb grabbed a flashlight and blanket and headed down a nearly hidden path.

"Watch your step."

Doreen gripped Zeb's hand tightly as he led her into a secluded area that allowed a clear view of the mountain lake. He spread the blanket for his lady as golden rays of twilight sneaked through the heavy growth of pines and lit the forest floor. Sparse beams of light flickering over low-lying ferns projected an illusion of fire painted onto the landscape. The dying sun reflected an orange hue on the lake's shimmering surface.

"It's so beautiful," sighed Doreen.

"Feel better?" he asked.

"A little bit," she replied.

The couple sat quietly on the woolen blanket. In the unfolding night sky, a solitary star caught Doreen's eye.

"Zeb, do you know the old children's rhyme. Star light, star bright."

"I wish I may I wish I might," added Zeb, joining with Doreen until they spoke as one voice.

"Have the wish I wish tonight."

Zeb inhaled Doreen's womanly fragrance. Overhead the single star gradually became millions of twinkling white specks as night emerged in the heavens.

"Do you believe in God? I mean really believe in God?" asked Doreen.

"Of course. Doesn't everyone?"

"What I mean is…did you ever have any doubt?"

"Sure, doesn't everyone?"

"Do you now?"

"Do I what?" asked Zeb. "Do I have any doubt now? Right now? Tonight?"

"Yes. At this very moment."

"Do you want to hear a little story?"

"Oh, Zeb, I would love that."

Snuggled in Zeb's warmth, Doreen felt as secure as she had in childhood when her parents told her a good night story. Listening to Zeb's soft regular breathing pattern, Doreen realized precisely what had been absent in her life. It was something she had not dared to think about for years. It was that sacred place in the heart where safety takes its rest. Her faith had been tested in ways that no one in Safford, Arizona could even imagine. Not even Zeb had a clue to the suffering she had undergone.

"About ten years ago I was wrestling with my belief system," said Zeb. "My faith in the world was at a real low point. I had done my time in the military where I saw things no one should have to see. I'd put in five years as a cop over in Tucson. One day I woke up and decided it was time to return home. Looking back on it, I probably wanted to show everybody I grew up with just how much of a man I had become. You might say I was riding a high and mighty horse. It was a time in my life when I was pretty good at shooting my mouth off. I said some pretty stupid things."

"What kind of stupid things?"

"You name it. I was a self-styled expert on everything from war to religion. I was so darn smart I could barely stand it myself. Then something happened and I got a lucky break."

"What happened?"

"A pair of angels landed on my shoulder."

"Angels?"

"Jake Dablo and Jimmy Song Bird decided to take me under their collective wing."

"Human angels you mean."

"Angels come in many forms."

"So does the devil," interjected Doreen. "So does the devil."

Zeb stopped and eyed her inquisitively. Her eyes told him to carry on with his story. He did but made a permanent mental note of Doreen's curious statement.

"I was working for Sheriff Dablo as his deputy. Sometimes we'd have the occasion to stop by Song Bird's place out on the San Carlos. As you know Jake and Song Bird go way back. I think mostly our trips out there were just a way for them to get together to jawbone. Song Bird would put on some sassafras tea..."

"Mmm, I love sassafras tea," cooed Doreen

"One day we were sitting around the kitchen table out at Song Bird's. I started yapping about how there just might not be a God. I suppose I was saying it just to shock them. I was real surprised when they didn't take me to task. Instead they just let it pass. They acted like they didn't hear my foolish rant. Then, about a week later, Jake asked me if I wanted to go fishing up here at Riggs Lake. I thought, sure, a little trout fishing sounded like a good idea."

"Look a shooting star!" cried Doreen.

"Make a wish."

"I already did," said Doreen, kissing Zeb on the neck.

"The Apaches believe a shooting star is an omen of an advancing enemy," said Zeb.

"Well, that's one thing they're wrong about then. Now go ahead, go on with your story. It's startin' to get real interesting."

"It was around sunset. We fished for an hour or so. I guess we caught a few rainbows, when over the hillside, right over there..." Zeb pointed toward the southern corner of the lake where a small dale and some pine trees nestled near the edge of the water. "Up walks Jimmy Song Bird. Right out of nowhere. He was wearing his Apache Medicine Man clothes. I swear to God, it looked like he was walking right across the lake on top of the water."

"Did he stop and talk to you and Jake?"

"You bet he did. Song Bird told us this story

about how sacred Mount Graham is to the Apaches. He explained how the Apaches believe the mountain spirits, the Ga'an, live here. The Ga'an provide the Apaches with strength against their enemies, fertility for their women, prosperity for their people, rain for their crops and plants to heal their sick. Song Bird said Mount Graham is the most important sacred mountain in the entire world according to the Apache way of thinking. Then Jake started adding his two cents. It didn't take long to realize my way of thinking was pretty small and narrow."

"What'd Jake say?"

"Jake grew up listening to his grandfather tell stories about the stars in the heavens. Just like we believe in God, Jake said the Greeks believed Zeus was the Supreme Being. The Romans believed the same about Jupiter. Zeus lived on Mount Olympus, just like the Ga'an live on Mount Graham. Jupiter lived above the mountaintop in the sky. Like the Ga'an, Zeus and Jupiter granted victory in war, protection for the people, good weather for sailors and rain for crops."

"That's cool stuff."

"I thought so too. Song Bird and Jake were sitting right about where we're sitting, and they agreed there was hardly a lick of difference between the Greeks, the Romans, the Apaches and the Christians when it came right down to it."

"When you think about it like that, I guess we're all pretty much the same."

"I learned everyone has their own view of the world. Ever since that day, I figured if every culture believes in a higher power, who was I to fight it? Besides, it feels better to have faith than to fight it."

"I know you're right, Zeb, but sometimes superstition gets the better of me."

"What do you mean, Doe?"

"Every time I get to believin' real strong... bang! Just like clockwork somethin' happens to test my faith."

"Are you talking about Father McNamara's suicide?"

"It wasn't a suicide," insisted Doreen. "But I am talking about death."

Once again it was obvious to Zeb that Doreen wanted to tell him something, but she was choosing to keep mum. Before he could pursue, it he heard the hiss of a newly started fire crackling near the edge of the lake. Zeb turned to see the outline of a smallish person leaning over, breaking twigs and placing them on a campfire.

"Someone's camping. It looks like they're building a fire. I'd better go over and let them know the fire danger level is high today."

"Ooh, do you have to?"

"I should warn them. A fire getting out of control up here would be big trouble. They could burn the whole mountain down. It'll just take a minute."

Zeb stood to get a better view. He took a few

steps toward their unexpected guest.

"Wait for me," cried Doreen. "I'm goin' with you."

Zeb extended his hands helping Doreen rise from the forest floor. His efforts were rewarded with a hug.

"Hello there," shouted Zeb.

A squeaky voice returned the greeting. Its high pitch made it impossible to tell if they were approaching a man or a woman.

"I saw you two sitting over there. I hope I'm not bothering you."

In the light of the campfire Zeb could see the stranger was a man. The sheriff's eyes were drawn to the man's camouflaged tent, a large cache of food slung over a tree branch and a piece of equipment covered by a bed sheet.

"My name is Venerable Bede," said the man, extending a hand to Sheriff Hanks.

The lack of calluses on the camper's hands told Zeb the man did not suffer under the strains of physical labor to earn his daily bread. His thick glasses made him look like a bookworm or a man with severe eye problems.

"I'm Sheriff Zeb Hanks. This is Doreen Nightingale."

"Pleased to meet the both of you. What can I do for you?

"It's about your campfire," said the sheriff. "It's illegal."

"You're not about to arrest me, are you?"

"No," laughed Zeb. "But I did want to let you know you should build your fire in one of the fire pits."

"I'm sorry," said Bede. "I'll take care of it right away."

"For tonight, just put some more rocks around the fire so it won't spread after you're asleep. You can move it in the morning."

"Thanks, I promise I will. I'm not one to break the law."

"I didn't quite catch your name. What was it again?"

"Bede, Doctor Venerable Bede."

Zeb didn't recognize the name.

"Are you from around here?"

"No."

"I didn't think so. I'd remember a name like Venerable Bede, if I'd heard it before."

"It's an unusual name. People always remark on it."

"What's a medical doctor doing out here?"

"I'm not an MD. I'm an environmental botanist, an ecologist really."

"Now just what the criminy sakes is that all about?" asked Doreen.

Bede chuckled.

"That's the same question I get from everyone. It's a relatively new field of study. My area of expertise is rare plants. It's not really that complicated. I find rare plants and study them in their natural surroundings. The idea, of course, is to save the species."

"What on earth can happen to a plant way out here?" asked Doreen.

"Some plants get over harvested when animal populations increase too rapidly. Fire destroys other plants. Some are simply overtaken by more dominant plants. It's nature's way. Lately my work is leading me to conclude that the real culprit is the homo sapien."

"Homo what?" asked Doreen.

"Man. Man destroys plants by moving into their natural habitat. The strongest plants always survive. Occasionally a weaker plant will survive by adapting and actually become the strongest. I study those survivors. My area of expertise is plants able to stand up against much stronger forces. I consider them my children, my babies. My job is to protect them against the evil that man can do."

Zeb glanced at Doreen out of the corner of his eye.

"So what brings you up to this neck of the woods?" asked the sheriff.

"I have a contract job with the Forest Service."

Satisfied everything was reasonably in order, Zeb stuck out his hand.

"Good enough. We'll be on our way. You might see me again, Dr. Bede. My work brings me up here occasionally."

"I'll be working up here for the next two months. I have quite a large amount of information to gather," replied Dr. Bede.

The three exchanged respective good nights and parted company. As Zeb turned his car around, the headlights flashed toward Dr. Bede who was removing the cloth sheet covering his equipment.

"Why did you tell that man you come up here often?" asked Doreen. "You told me it's been a long time since you been up here."

Zeb's lack of a quick response answered her question.

"You were checking up on that guy, weren't you? You was wonderin' how long he was going to be around?"

"Yup."

"Why?"

"I'm the sheriff, that's why. Plus that statement he made about the plants being his children. Don't tell me that didn't strike you as a little odd?"

"He's different lookin' enough all right with that rounded back of his and those funny glasses. But he ain't what you'd call dangerous unless he sets out to scratch someone."

"Scratch someone?"

"Didn't you notice his fingernails? They were long, manicured like he was fresh from one of them fancy makeovers the rich women get."

"I missed his nails, but there was something that made me wonder about him."

"You think that skinny little egghead looked

suspicious? What kind of trouble could he be? He looks like a man who couldn't kick his way out of a wet paper bag even if he was wearin' pointy-toed boots. Land sakes alive, he was about five foot six and couldn't have weighed more than a hundred forty pounds drippin' wet in his undies. That lil' ol' boy couldn't hurt a flea if he tried."

"I suppose you're right. He is a bit of a flea flicker, but he had a firm grip."

"Zeb, if I decide to marry you, would you promise to shut down the sheriff's side of your brain every once in a while and give it a rest?"

Overhead a full moon floated over the desert floor, suspended between heaven and earth.

"All you have to do is say yes," he said.

CHAPTER SEVEN

"Sheriff Hanks."

The stern vocal intonations of his strict Mormon secretary perked Sheriff Hanks' ears. Helen Nazelrod came huffing into his office with an oversized armload of paperwork.

"Why, come right in, Helen."

The sheriff's semi-sarcastic response was lost on his secretary who had already scooted five feet past the doorway and was now standing in front of his desk.

"What's on your mind?"

"It's not what's on my mind. It's what's not on yours."

Sheriff Hanks scratched his head as he looked at the stack of papers his exasperated secretary had slapped on his desk.

"What's all this?"

"Well, Romeo, ever since you took that trip up the mountain last week with your girlfriend, you seem to have forgotten about your job."

With the recent increase in his social activities, Sheriff Hanks couldn't deny he had been letting his record-keeping lag. But he knew it was not the paperwork that was bugging his secretary. It was the simple fact he was dating a Catholic woman, a Catholic woman who spent little time inside the church. To Helen mind he was betraying a fundamental Mormon tenet by dating outside the faith.

"These all need your signature."

Helen harrumphed as she took the top third of the stack and smacked it down on his desk.

"And these are from the courthouse. They need to be delivered to various offices. I'm sure you can figure out where."

A second pile stood stacked on the sheriff's desk.

"These, well, these I don't know what you want done with. Some things you're just going to have to figure out on your own."

Helen pulled an envelope seemingly out of midair. She dropped it atop the pile.

"Doc Yackley sent this over."

Zeb fingered the envelope. Helen stomped toward the door. Halfway out she turned to say one more thing. Her voice was somewhat calmer.

"Jake Dablo called to remind you about the planning commission meeting tonight. It's at seven."

"Thanks, Helen," replied the sheriff. "I think."

Sheriff Hanks rotated his wrist eyeing his watch. Five o'clock. He could probably reduce the work to a reasonable level by quarter to seven if he skipped his intended dinner at the Town Talk.

Outside his door Helen drummed her fingernails loudly, impatiently waiting for him to return some of the work so she could complete any follow-up.

Sheriff Hanks picked up the phone and dialed

Doreen.

"Town Talk, home of the world famous Tex-Mex burger. If you like 'em in singles, you'll love 'em in pairs. And don't forget, we do the dishes."

"Doe, its Zeb."

"Hello there, sugar dumplin'. My vibes was just wanderin' in your direction."

"Really?" said Zeb hopefully.

"You bet yer bottom dollar."

"What kinds of thoughts were crossing your mind?"

"My head was tellin' me that you ain't stayed late at the office for weeks. Are you takin' the job of sheriff of Graham County seriously, or are you not?"

"Did Helen call you?"

"Let's just say it don't take long for the prattle of wiggle-wagglin' tongues to land itself upon my ears."

"It sure doesn't."

"Just cuz' you got your mind on little ol' me doesn't mean you should be slackin' off everywhere else. You gotta remember always that you're a duly elected official."

"But you're forgetting one little thing, Doe."

"Not likely."

"You're the one who told me not to work twenty-four hours a day."

"But, honey bun, if you spend your time tom cattin' around like some ol' stray sniffin' heat and don't get your work done what are folks around here gonna think of me?"

"Well, actually, that's what I'm calling about. I've got a mountain of paperwork to do, and I promised Jake I would sit in on a county commission meeting tonight. So I won't be able to get by to see you until way late."

"That's good enough by me, but don't think for one minute that I won't sure enough miss you til' you're layin' by my side. Say, what's old Jake need you at a meeting for? Somebody expecting some trouble?"

"Nothing that exciting."

"What is it then?"

Zeb could tell Doreen was on a fishing expedition for a new round of gossip fodder.

"Aliens. We're expecting little green men from outer space to land on Mount Graham. You have to promise not to tell everyone."

"Hush your mouth, Sheriff Zebulon Hanks. If you don't watch your tongue, you might just find yourself lookin' for a new piece of arm candy."

"Hey, come on, Doe. I was just kidding."

"You just go on and take care of your business. And if any of them Martians show up at the commission meeting, send 'em on over to the Town Talk. We could use a little excitement around here tonight."

"You're too cute."

"You just say that cause you're sweet on me."

"Like frosting on cake."

"Now I could sit here all night listenin' to that

kinda talk but I gotta run, hon'. There's a lotta' hungry cowboys chompin' at the bit for some homemade chow."

"Doe, before you go. I just got a note from Doc Yackley on the post mortem blood tests on Father McNamara."

"Yes?"

"The preliminary tests are normal, but something Doc called a generic marker for toxins was off just a little. He's checking into it a bit further."

"What's that mean?"

"I don't know. Maybe nothing."

"But maybe something?"

"Maybe. I can't really say."

"I know he didn't kill himself. I wish I could get you to see it through my eyes. Then you would know," said Doreen.

Zeb got some work done and hustled to the meeting. John Farrell had already called the gathering to order by the time he arrived. Jake caught Zeb's eye. They exchanged slight head nods as he sneaked in the back and took a chair. Force of habit led Zeb to survey the room. Besides the five commissioners two other people were present at the open meeting. One was the widow, Norma Jane Jertson. Everyone knew her as a notorious busy body who made it her personal business to attend all of the commission meetings in homage to her dead husband, Earl. Earl had served on the commission for the better part of the past four decades. The gossipy widow, a controlling woman, had never let poor Earl out of her sight. Jake had joked that Norma Jane attended the meetings because she had it figured if old Earl was to come back from the dead, it would be the first place he would show up.

The other attendee was a short, thin, middle-aged man with a rounded back. From where he sat, in the shadowed corner of the room, Zeb couldn't see the man's face. Something about the small man appeared vaguely familiar.

"The first order of business is."

John Farrell started the meeting with his usual air of pomposity. As the board chairman droned on, Zeb absent-mindedly looked about the room. It took his best effort to pay attention to the long-winded Farrell. He found himself wondering what Mrs. Jertson would do if her former husband actually did come back from the dead.

After a time his eyes landed on the round-shouldered stranger. He appeared to be taking notes. The man began to look vaguely familiar. It dawned on Zeb the visitor was none other than Dr. Venerable Bede. When Bede reached back and rubbed his neck, Zeb noticed the manicure job and long fingernails Doreen had earlier pointed out to him.

Bede must have sensed the heat of the sheriff's stare. He turned and looked directly at Zeb. Caught in the act, Zeb returned the doctor's gaze with a crinkled smile and a slight wave.

"The last order of regular business shouldn't take more than one or two minutes of our time. Then we can all go home and call it a night," said Farrell. "The final order of business is a request for a conditional use permit for thirty-five acres of land. This land is officially designated by the county as plat six-one-six-six. The owner of the land is a public non-profit corporation known as AIMGO. They request permission to place the land in question into an Arizona Land Trust in perpetuity. In order to assure the county and state of its good intention as owner of the property, the corporation agrees to assign all rights of trust to the Forest Service of the United States of America of an additional one hundred acres that immediately surrounds the aforementioned thirty-five acres. If there are no objections, would someone care to offer up a motion?"

Jake cleared his throat loudly. A hushed quiet came over the room as all eyes turned to the ex-sheriff.

"Yes, Jake, what is it?"

The tone of the chairman's voice was clearly that of irritation.

"I was wondering where county plat six-one-six-six is? Exactly, I mean."

"It's one of those plots of unused land. My guess is that the organization probably wants to use it for a camp. One of the owners is the Catholic Church. For God's sake, what harm can they do?"

The immediate overreaction by Farrell raised the hackles on Jake's neck.

"I'm not suggesting any intended harm. I just want to know where plat number six-one-six-six is located before I vote on the resolution."

"Jesus, Jake, it's a large county..."

"I know, John, lived here all my life."

Jake shot a sideways glance toward Sheriff Hanks. Zeb got the message.

"Let me see here," mumbled Chairman Farrell, shuffling some neatly stacked papers in front of him into disarray. "This may take a minute."

"Take your time. A few more minutes on a long night won't harm any of us."

Jake crossed his arms, leaned back in the chair and waited. Several long silent minutes passed before the exasperated Farrell finally grumbled sharply.

"It's near the top of Mount Graham. Does that answer your question?"

Jake's suspicions were confirmed. The other commissioners who seemed to have been paying little attention suddenly became alert. Norma Jane Jertson placed her knitting needles in her lap and took out a notepad. Even Doctor Bede seemed to shift side to side in his seat with apparent increased interest.

"You say the group of people who own this property, including the Catholic Church, have made it clear they want to use the area for a camp?

Did I understand that to be part of the resolution?"

"Something along those lines. They haven't said exactly. But, like I said, what trouble can the Catholic Church possibly bring us?"

The smug, condescending tone of Farrell's voice irritated Jake.

"Besides the church, who else is named on the deed of ownership?"

"I don't know. I just know that the permit request stated there were multiple owners incorporated under the name of AIMGO."

"How do you know the Catholic Church is one of them?"

"I sold one of the tracts of land to a representative of the Catholic Church. The check for the property was from the local Catholic Diocese. It's all a matter of public record."

Sheriff Hanks observed the small audience. Mrs. Jertson was taking notes at such a furious pace she knocked her knitting needles onto the floor and didn't even bother to stop and pick them up. The board members fidgeted uncomfortably. But it was Dr. Bede's bulging neck veins that gave Zeb pause.

"Don't you think it would behoove us to find out who the other owners are before we give them the use permit?" asked Jake.

"I trust the Catholic Church. Don't you?"

"Can't say as I do. Can't say as I don't. But any one person's trust in the church is hardly what this is all about."

"Well then," proposed Farrell. "I move we vote on the resolution. Does anyone second the motion?"

A mouse scurrying across the floor would have sent an echo through the quiet room.

"Since there seem to be no seconds to the motion, I move we table the motion until we gather further information," stated Jake.

His motion was quickly seconded and voted on. The vote was four to one, Farrell in the minority.

"I volunteer to look into AIMGO and find out who the other members are," explained Jake.

Heads nodded in agreement.

"You're just wasting your time, Jake," said Farrell, gavel in hand. "Take my advice and leave it alone."

"I'll have a full report for the next regularly scheduled meeting," replied Jake.

Farrell angrily banged his gavel.

"Meeting adjourned."

CHAPTER EIGHT

Outside the meeting Sheriff Hanks called out to Dr. Bede. He was making his way toward a massive pickup truck that seemed out of character for someone like him.

"Dr. Bede," hailed the sheriff.

"Sheriff Hanks? I didn't recognize you in your uniform."

Dr. Bede squinted through the thick lenses of his bifocals.

"What brings you around to a planning commission meeting?"

"Sheriff, this may sound a little strange, but I was bored so when I came across a notice in the paper about a public meeting, I thought I'd attend. It's kind of a hobby of mine."

"A hobby?"

"Yes, you see, with my work I'm away from home quite a bit of the time. I'm not much for sitting in front of the television. The movies these days are too violent. So I've made it a hobby to attend local meetings wherever I go. It helps pass the time."

"That's, uh, interesting."

"You'd be surprised what you can learn about a community from attending meetings."

"Oh, I'm sure. Did you enjoy the meeting?"

"It got a little testy there at the end. It made me

a little nervous."

Sheriff Hanks looked up to see Jake Dablo coming toward them.

"Jake, I've got someone here I'd like you to meet."

"Zeb, thanks for coming to the meeting. Who's your friend?"

"Jake, this is Dr. Venerable Bede."

"Pleased to meet you."

Zeb eyed Jake's facial expression as Bede's soft hand disappeared into Jake's gnarly fingers.

"I saw you at the meeting. It was nice to have someone other than old Mrs. Jertson around. I swear to God I've watched her knit enough booties to cover a family of octopuses."

"Octopi," corrected Bede.

"Dr. Bede makes it his hobby to attend local town meetings," said Zeb.

"Interesting way to pass the time," said Jake. "What do you do for real work?"

"Actually, I'm a botanical consultant. I've been doing some work for the Forest Service on the upper elevations of Mount Graham."

"A botanical consultant? I can't say as I've ever heard of that particular occupation before. But I guess it figures a federal agency would have a few on staff."

Jake's humor was lost on the doctor.

"What sort of botanical consulting are you doing up on Mount Graham?" asked Jake.

"Surveying, identifying and cataloging unusual

and rare plants. Mount Graham is really quite a natural wonder."

Jake and Zeb listened politely as Dr. Bede recited a litany of minor subspecies of plants unique to the area. He explained how the unusual proximity of the five distinct ecological life zones on the mountain created a rare opportunity for plant cross-pollination. This combination of circumstances led to entirely unique breeds of plants that likely existed nowhere else on the planet, a planet Bede was apparently bent on saving.

"You know, Doc, if you want to learn some traditional lore surrounding Mount Graham, you might want to head out to the San Carlos Reservation on Saturday night. Jimmy Song Bird, an Apache Medicine Man, is giving a little educational talk on how Apaches view the mountain. It's for the tribal members, but it's open to the public."

"Well, thank you. I think I'd enjoy that a great deal. It sounds fascinating."

"Put it on your calendar."

"I will and thank you for letting me know about it. I should be on my way now. I'm camping up on Mount Graham. I don't much like to drive too long after dark if I don't have to. I bid you gentlemen goodnight."

Jake and Zeb watched as the doctor stepped up into the large pickup with dual tires on the rear axle.

"What do you think?" asked Jake.

"About Farrell's little tizzy when you questioned his plan of action?"

"Yup."

"He seemed a little upset. Maybe a little more than he should have been," replied Zeb.

"I suspect he's not used to anyone questioning his authority," said Jake. "Since I've been on the commission, no one ever has had any reason to stand up to him."

"Maybe this deal is a moneymaker for him," said Zeb. "With him it's all business."

"Doesn't it seem strange to you the Catholic Church and its cohorts would quietly buy a bunch of land through foreclosures using a dummy corporation?" asked Jake.

"I don't know. Why not? The Catholic Church is just like any church. Just like the Mormon Church. They own a lot of land. Nothing illegal about that."

"Damn it, Zeb. Doesn't it seem strange that a religious organization would do the whole deal so quietly? It's almost as if they're trying to sneak it by someone."

"Like they had something else in mind for the land?"

"Exactly," replied Jake.

"You're a lawman, Jake. Some sort of proof wouldn't be such a bad idea, now would it?"

"I'm working on that. You have to admit it was odd how Farrell got all worked up when I questioned him about what was going on with the property. He took it personally."

"It could be that you are reading a little too much into this, Jake. Look at it from his point of view. Maybe he thinks you're up to something. Maybe he thinks you are trying to cut him out of a real estate commission."

"Hogwash!! I know a skunk when I smell one. So should you."

"Take it easy, Jake. I just want to make sure you're seeing things clearly. So what do you want me to do?"

"Nothing for the time being. I just wanted you to witness the goings on in case something comes up in the future."

"Just what the hell do you really think is going on?" asked the sheriff.

"That's the trouble, Zeb. I don't know. I just don't know. But you can bet your damn boots I'm going to snoop around until I'm satisfied."

"I'm not saying I agree with the way you see this, but is there anything in particular you'd like me to be on the lookout for?"

"You know it just dawned on me. There is something you can do."

"What's that?" asked Zeb.

"You can ask Deputy Delbert to talk to that little old lady who lives next door to him. What's her name? Mrs. Espinoza?"

"Yeah, that's right. Mrs. Espinoza."

"She was Father McNamara's housekeeper,

wasn't she?"

"Right. She's been the housekeeper over at the Saint Barnabus' rectory forever," said Zeb.

"Then I'll just bet she knows every little secret that ever went on inside that house."

"I'd say there's a pretty good chance of that. But what sort of secrets could a priest's house hold? What makes you think she'll spill the dirty secrets, if there are any?"

"Good questions. Does Delbert ever talk with her?"

"Delbert talks with everybody. You can't shut him up. You know that."

"In a roundabout way, why don't you try and see if Mrs. Espinoza ever said anything to Delbert about the church and land up on Mount Graham."

"What sort of information are you looking for?" asked Zeb.

"Oh, I don't know exactly. Maybe someone left the parish some land up there. Perhaps there were dealings going on with Father McNamara and the diocese about land on the mountain. I'm looking for anything that might link Saint Barnabus or the late Father McNamara with what's going on up there."

"Once a sheriff, always a sheriff, eh' Jake? I swear sometimes you get an idea so stuck in your head a stick of dynamite couldn't shake it loose."

Ex-sheriff Jake Dablo looked over at his one-time understudy. Somewhere deep inside his gut an alarm bell was ringing. Jake knew the inevitable downfall of every lawman was a cocksure attitude. He was beginning to sense that in Zeb. Jake also had lived long enough to know there wasn't a damn thing he could do to save another man from his personal destiny.

"Once it's in your blood, it's got nowhere else to go but through your veins," said Jake, turning away and spitting on the ground.

Jake's body language told Zeb he'd offended his ex-boss.

"Did I say something to piss you off?"

"Nope."

"What then?"

"I'd hate to see something happen to you or one of your people because you quit paying attention."

"You talking about something in particular?" asked the sheriff.

"Nope. Let's just say my gut is talking to me."

Jake Dablo ambled over to his old pickup truck and stuck the key in the ignition. It grumbled, spit a bit and backfired twice before lunging into forward gear.

Sheriff Hanks watched the aging man in his old rust bucket of a truck head down the road.

Was Jake right? Was there something he wasn't paying attention to?

CHAPTER NINE

"What's going on around here? Did the whole town lose its appetite at once?"

Kate Steele approached the back counter of the Town Talk Diner where Doreen Nightingale was hunched over a disorganized stack of invoices.

"Too late for breakfast, too early for coffee break," replied Doreen. "Can I get you something?"

"Stay seated. Finish your book work. I can serve myself. I wasn't always a Deputy Sheriff, you know. I worked my way through college as a waitress."

"I declare, from the first time I met you I knew you had somethin' special about ya. But I never did figure you for bein' the waitress type."

"I like to say my undergraduate degree is in waitressology."

"Oooh, wee, I like the sounds of that," said Doreen. "Kind of elevates the profession a notch or two, if you know what I mean."

"Things have been so slow at the sheriff's office this week that I might just ask for a part-time job around here," said Kate. "I've got to do something to keep me from going stir crazy."

"Zeb said things were real slow in the police business. Crooks and thieves take a holiday is what he called it. He claims it's got to do with Father McNamara's death."

"You mean his theory that riffraff and men of the cloth are just flip sides of the same coin? And that criminals feel low when a religious man dies so they take a little time off?" asked Kate.

"Zeb believes priests and ministers treat crooks like regular folks. I guess it only goes to figure that when a religious man dies, the bad guys lay low out of respect," said Doreen, a tear welling in her eye. "Father McNamara, he understood people and problems like no one else."

"Father McNamara had the common touch and Zeb's a good lawman. Top cops like him spend a whole lot of time figuring out criminal behavioral patterns. It's like putting pieces of a puzzle together," explained Kate. "What you working on?"

"A jigsaw puzzle of my own, the never ending process of juggling the books. Today for example, just when I figure I got the income and the outgo all evened up, I realize the egg man has been muckin' up the works."

"How can that be?" asked Kate. "Everyone says Chicken Jimmy is the most honest man in Safford."

"He is, sort of. But he's got his own way of monkey wrenchin'. Every time I order a dozen dozen eggs he throws in a thirteenth dozen for nothing. Problem is he never bothered to tell lil' ol' me what he was up to. Long story short, my inventory is all screwed up. When I asked the old buzzard what he was up to, he acted like he didn't know what I was talkin' about. He looked at me like I was a little bit off my nut."

"The old guy probably has a little crush on you, Doreen. It's hardly a crime when someone cheats you in your favor."

"Be that as it may, I've done got it figured on how to get even with the old rascal."

"What's your plan?"

"I'm gonna trick him by underchargin' him for his meals," laughed Doreen. "Your coffee still good and fresh? I can brew you up a fresh batch if you want."

"It's fine. I just wanted one quick cup before I head out to the San Carlos."

"What takes you out that way?" asked Doreen. "Not trouble I hope?"

"No. I've got to locate an elderly woman by the name of Beulah Trees."

"Is old Beulah still alive? I woulda thought she died years ago. She must be a hundred years old by now."

"As a matter of fact she is exactly one hundred years old according to tribal records."

Sensing impending gossip, Doreen put down her pencil. She began fidgeting with her hair. The updo, a cross between a beehive and a bun, was adorned with a single string of leather ringed with multi-colored beads. A silver clip shaped like an American flag with a Day-Glo peace symbol topped it off.

"Whatcha' gotta find Beulah for?"

"I'm delivering a court ordered foreclosure notice."

"Out on the Rez? Now that don't figure to add up. What's the skinny?"

"Beulah's mother got some land years ago when the federal government confiscated her land for mineral rights. They leased out the rights to a mining company."

"You mean the government could come right in and kick an Indian off reservation land?" asked Doreen.

"Pretty much."

"How in the name of kingdom come could they get away with such a thing? I thought the Rez belonged to the Indians."

"It does, but the federal government can do pretty much whatever it pleases."

"So if they kick Indians off their reservation land, what do the Indians get in return?"

Kate explained the process briefly.

"There have been times when the Native American refused the government's money. In those cases the government deeded them land of equal value."

"How's that work?"

"Usually the land was out in the middle of nowhere with no roads going to it and no water on it."

"Sounds as crooked as a bent walkin' stick."

"It was all done legally. Ethically, that's a horse of a different color. In the end, after the mines played out, all that was left was a big hole in the ground."

"Hard to believe, ain't it," said Doreen. "I mean that the federal government could do such a thing legally. So what's this got to do with Beulah again?"

"Way back when, her mother was given land on the upper elevations of Mount Graham in return for the reservation land they took for the mineral rights. Of the sixty or seventy tracts of land up on Mount Graham involved in the land and mineral rights deal, most of them ended up like hers, foreclosed upon."

"Foreclosed on? Why?"

"It was one of those confusing and poorly thought out federal government programs. Tribal members don't pay property taxes on reservation property. When the government gave them land off the reservation, the agreement allowed the first generation of Native Americans living on the 'off reservation' land to be exempt from property taxes."

"Sounds fair enough."

"Here's the problem. Only the first generation was exempt from the taxes. Their children and heirs weren't."

"So what happened?"

"The 'no property tax deal' wasn't explained all that well to the Native Americans."

"Ain't that a shock," said Doreen facetiously.

"A lot of people didn't have any idea they

owed taxes on their land. Almost all of the descendants of the first generation just assumed the land was treated like reservation land. They figured no taxes were owed on it."

"And if you don't pay your taxes, you lose your land, right?"

"Exactly right," replied Kate.

"Lord, but that don't seem right considerin' the circumstances."

"Eskadi says it's all part of an ongoing conspiracy by the federal government against all Native American people. I don't always stand on his side of the fence, but when you think about it in this case, he might be right."

Kate further explained that county officials would wait five or ten years before they tried to collect any taxes. By then, with penalties tacked on, the amount owed usually was more than the property was worth. The county would file a tax lien against the property. If the owner didn't pay it, the land would go on the auction block.

"What happened to the people living on the property?"

"Most of the property was never lived on. Almost all of the people who got kicked off their land when the mining companies came in moved in with relatives somewhere else on the San Carlos Reservation. Besides, most Apaches would never live on Mount Graham."

"Why not? The land was given to them fair and square."

"Apaches believe that Mount Graham is a fundamental sacred site, a sacred home of the Gods. Being that it's a holy place, people aren't supposed to live up there."

"Any Apaches besides Beulah still own land up there?"

"I think only three pieces of privately owned Apache property are left. Surprisingly two of them are homesteaded. Beulah owns the third, but, according to the records, she has never lived on it. I'm not so sure she even knows about it."

"You said two plots of land are still owned by Indians?"

"Yes. Both of the owners have close ties to the San Carlos."

"You know quite a lot about this, don't ya, Katie?"

"I've been learning. The two parcels of land are near each other. One of them is right up by Riggs Lake. It's near the top of the mountain."

"Ya' don't say. I know that lake. Zeb took me up there. It is a beautiful place."

"The other one is not far from there. It's near Ladybug Saddle."

"Heck, I know about that spot too. Zeb told me last summer during ladybug season some of the trees' trunks up there were turned orange from all the ladybugs. Zeb said some old hermit lives up there somewhere."

"That's right. His name is Ramon Hickman. He's one of the two Apaches who owns land and lives up there. I hear he only comes to town maybe once a year. The Apaches consider him almost sacred in a sense because of his way."

"His way?" asked Doreen. "What way is that?"

"The tribal elders call it the 'quiet way' because he hardly ever talks."

"How come the cat got his tongue?"

"It's quite a story. He's a Christian Apache, but he follows all the old ways too. He got religion during the war. Nobody knows for sure. Some say he took a vow to only talk if had to because of an experience during the war."

"What the heck happened?"

"According to local legend, he was captured. When he wouldn't talk, he was tortured. They threatened to cut out his tongue."

"Cut out his tongue! Who captured him?"

"The Nazis."

"What a terrible thing. What else do you know about it?"

"The Apache people don't like to talk about it. They believe it's bad luck to retell a hard luck story. As I understand it, they think if you repeat a story about someone's misfortune, it can bounce back and cause the same thing to happen to you."

"I suppose it could be true. Ya' never know how them things work. What do you know about Hickman's story?"

"What I've heard was that Hickman was a military courier. His job was to carry information between battlefield commanders. It's said he could run all day and all night without ever tiring."

"Well, I'll be dipped. That's quite a talent."

"They say one night he was captured. He hid the papers he was carrying, just like he was ordered to do. The Nazis threatened to cut out his tongue when he refused to tell them where he had stashed the documents. He still wouldn't talk. Then his captors lined up some innocent children and threatened to gun them down unless he told them what they wanted to know."

"Did he sing?"

"No, he didn't. He kept his mouth shut for two reasons. One, he was under orders. Two, he could not even begin to believe they would do something like that to innocent children."

"Did they kill the kids?"

"Yes, and they made him watch the whole thing."

"No way."

"That night he escaped. He just stood up and walked away. He didn't even care if the enemy killed him. When he got back to his troops and told them what happened, his commanding officer decided he was loco. He was labeled a 'Crazy Injun' and was given a section eight discharge."

"Section eight?"

"It's a way the military gets rid of people they decide have mental problems."

"That's terrible!"

"When he returned to the reservation, he went

through a Purification Ceremony. The Medicine Man had a vision that Ramon should live on Mount Graham. Up there he could be nearer the Gods and safer. Eskadi told me Ramon doesn't talk to anyone, not even the elders from the San Carlos who take him food and supplies and leave it near his cave."

"He lives in a cave? C'mon, Katie. This tale is getting' a little tall, even for the likes of me."

"It may be tall but it's true. The Elders of the tribe have no doubt the mountain spirits, the Ga'an, keep an eye on him."

"No kidding."

"They believe because of what happened to him he needs to be watched over. The Ga'an protect his path in this life because he suffers from having seen the horror of what happened to those children. It makes him strangely blessed in the Apache way of thinking."

"I suspect he's earned the right to have those Gods lookin' over his shoulder. What about the other one? You said two Apaches are living up on the Mount."

"The other is an ancient Medicine Man. His name is Geronimo Star in the Night. He's a traditional healer. He has a sweat lodge in a place the Apaches have considered a sacred holy place for over four hundred years. They say he has the gift of seeing the future."

"How the sam hill do you know so much about the goin's on up on the mountain?"

Kate finished her coffee and went behind the counter to refill her cup. Doreen fiddled with her hair, puffing her bangs.

"Want some?" asked Kate, holding up the coffeepot.

"Sure, pour me up. Dang, it feels funny to get waited on in your own place. Muchos gracias."

"No problem, you deserve it. You're a hard working woman."

"You know I sort of feel like I'm a kid again, sittin' and talkin' like this. My sister and I used to stay up late at night, listening to the radio, talking and telling stories, sharing secrets."

"You were blessed to have that."

"Yes, I was. I guess I forget that sometimes. Now back to what I was askin' you about? How in the name of kingdom come do you know so much about the mountain?"

"Eskadi has been mentoring me."

"Well, lo and behold and wonder of wonders. You can tickle my feet and paint me pink," cried Doreen, clapping her hands together in great delight.

"What?" laughed Kate. "Whatever do you mean?"

"Whatever do you mean?" aped Doreen. "I'm talkin' bout the first time you two ever done laid eyes on one another. I seen the sparks aflyin'. You'd have to be blind as a bat not to have."

"Yes," said Kate. "It was right here at this counter."

"Yer dang tootin'," said Doreen. "You were sittin' right here with my man, the good sheriff of Graham County, during one of your frequent coffee breaks…"

"…in walks this handsome Apache man with beautiful onyx colored eyes and jet black hair in a ponytail hanging down to the middle of his back. I thought he was some businessman from Phoenix or a college professor or maybe some mysterious stranger," added Kate.

Kate giggled like a teenager, realizing she could trust Doreen with the secrets of her love life. Doreen's eyes twinkled.

"He's a good lookin' man."

"You don't know the half of it," said Kate.

"And it's a damn good thing I don't or you might have some competition. Since you're travelin' down memory lane, tell me just one more thing," said Doreen.

"Okay. I can do that," said Kate.

"Tell me exactly what you was wearin'."

Doreen's mysterious question gave Kate pause.

"I was on duty, so obviously I was in my uniform."

"That's not what I'm talkin' about. I swear to God, girl, there's a part of you missin' when it comes to usin' yer noodle like a woman. I mean what scent were you wearin'?"

Kate gave the worldly waitress a confused look and shook her head.

"Scent? What scent? What are you talking

about?"

"You were wearin'... Come on girl. Use your head as something other than a spot to rest yer deputy sheriff's hat."

"Let me see. What scent was I wearing? Sandalwood oil, that's it. Of course you would remember. It was a gift from you."

"That's what you think."

"What do you mean 'that's what I think?' You gave it to me. I remember when you handed it to me."

"And hon', what exactly is it that you remember?" Doreen's sassy tongue wagged like an impudent teenager.

"I remember your gift of the sandalwood oil very clearly because you told me it was a magic potion. There you go."

"And what makes you think a little ol' hash slingin' hussy like me would know the very first doggone thing about how to whip up a magic potion?"

"What are you saying?"

"The sandalwood oil was a magic potion made especially for you, but not by me. I was just the delivery gal."

"What on earth are you talking about?"

"You don't know what I'm talkin' about, do ya', hon'? I swear you were at the back of the line when the good Lord handed out female instincts."

"What are you talking about, Doe?"

"What I'm tellin' you, dearie, is that the

sandalwood oil was given to me to give to you."

"Why? By whom? For what reason?"

"By Jimmy Song Bird."

"Jimmy Song Bird?"

"You don't know what I'm gettin' at, do you?"

"I'm lost."

Deputy Kate Steele suddenly felt weak in the knees.

"Then I guess I'd be beholdin' to let the cat out of the bag now, wouldn't I."

"Please do."

"Son of a gun," sighed Doreen. "Talk about relief. I've been bustin' a gut for near a year tryin' to keep myself from spoutin' off about the whole dang deal. But I made a promise, and yours truly, if nothin' else in this vale of tears, is a loyal puppy dog when it comes to keepin' her promises."

Doreen walked behind the counter and refilled both of the cups with a freshly brewed pot of black coffee.

"Cream?"

"Just a smidgen."

Doreen smiled slyly as she poured cream into Kate's coffee cup.

"Are you going to tell me or am I going to have to arrest you to get a confession?"

"I can tell you the secret, only now, because I promised Song Bird. Actually, he made me promise that I wouldn't say nothin' until you figured it out first. I guess he musta had his reasons, but for the life of me I can't figure out what they'd be."

"Good Lord, Doe, you sure can take a long time getting to a point."

"So I've been told. Everybody knows that most of the fun ain't in the arrivin' but is in the gettin' where you're goin'."

Doreen scooted back around the counter, sat down next to her friend, and looked at her face to face, eye to eye, friend to friend.

"When your daddy was dyin'," began Doreen.

A wave of joy peppered with sadness rushed through Kate. Memories came flooding back as she thought of her father in his final days, slowly dying from cancer as he lay like a helpless child on his tattered sofa. In those bittersweet final days of his life, father and daughter bid farewell in a thousand gentle ways. Her father talked with her at length about how the Medicine Men, Jimmy Song Bird and Geronimo Star in the Night, had prepared him for his unknown journey. They taught him that his fate was to return to his ancestors. The wise practitioners led him down a path of enlightenment and awareness as his transition to the next world slowly became a reality. When he slipped peacefully from his living body, thanks to the Medicine Men, Kate was given a uniquely powerful yet somehow strangely beautiful view of death.

"When he was makin' his preparations, in the way Apaches do," said Doreen. "In the old ways I mean, with the Medicine Men..."

Kate's thoughts flashed to a moonlit night outside of Geronimo Star in the Night's sweat lodge near the top of Mount Graham. Inside, the Medicine Men were helping her father prepare for his journey to the spirit world. As a woman she was not allowed to participate in the ceremony, but her heart was with her father.

"…one of the things your father asked Jimmy Song Bird to do was…well, he didn't actually ask him to do it."

"What did my father want of Jimmy Song Bird?" asked Kate.

"It was more of a wish actually," said Doreen. "He wished you would have the great gift of love like he and your mother had."

Tears from the infinitely deep well of human emotion welled in the eyes of Kate and Doreen. Neither woman made any attempt to ebb the flow.

"Jimmy Song Bird made a magic potion out of sandalwood oil. He give it to me to give to you. It was your father's final gift to you," said Doreen.

Kate's spirit soared in the transcendent realization that the love in her heart was unbound by the worldly constraints of life and death. It was her father's passing that brought her back to the Southwest, to a life she loved. Now she realized while preparing her father for his death, the old Medicine Men of the Apache tribe had also helped prepare her for life.

CHAPTER TEN

Kate Steele tingled with a sense of nervous anticipation as she dressed for her date with Eskadi Black Robes. Dabbing a touch of sandalwood oil behind each ear, she spoke to herself in the mirror.

"It's not really a date. It's more like another cultural lesson." She paused. "Who am I kidding? My feelings for Eskadi are getting stronger and stronger."

Eskadi's private tutoring in the traditional ways of the Apache was slowly beginning to give her an understanding of what it meant to be an Athabaskan, an Apache. Tonight, when Song Bird addressed the public gathering and gave the oral history of Mount Graham, Eskadi would be by her side.

Kate pulled her shiny, black hair into a ponytail, accenting her favorite abalone necklace and lapis earrings. Gazing at her reflection in the mirror, her sea green eyes sparkled with delight as she thought about Eskadi. Heading toward the reservation, she let her mind ponder the 'what ifs' of her life.

At the tribal center, she stepped out of the car to the steady pulse of rhythmic drumming. Her skin warmed as the deep harmony of chanting male voices reached her ears. Four half-asleep reservation mutts were lying on the ground in the parking lot. They lazily opened their eyes in acknowledgment of her arrival. Eskadi had explained to her that these dogs were part of the intricate harmony of all living things. He believed they were not unlike people. Some were good and others were bad. Some were so fat they could barely carry their own body weight. Others were so skinny a strong wind could push them over. They also had personalities. Some were kind. Others were as ornery as a knotted piece of wood beneath the saw blade. But, just like people, the dogs were living beings, so they should be given respect.

Eskadi had taught her to observe the animals by what he called the lesson of looking. Kate was tilting her head to make eye contact with a particularly mangy looking mutt when she felt the soft touch of a human hand on her shoulder. Her heart raced.

"Eskadi, you surprised me."

"I was watching you having a staring contest with Jingles. I figured if I didn't intervene, he was going to get the better of you," laughed Eskadi.

"Jingles?"

"He got hit in the head by a car when he was a puppy. He lost his sense of direction. The kids tied a bell around his neck so they could find him when he wandered off. Now he's old. He doesn't get lost anymore because he doesn't go any further than the back of the building."

"Is he your dog?"

"He's everybody's dog. Come on, let's get going. The story telling is about to begin."

"How do you know?"

"Weren't you listening to the drumming?"

"Of course I heard it."

"You heard the drumming, but you weren't listening. From watching your interaction with Jingles I know you are learning to see. Now you need to learn the art of listening."

In the near distance people were gathering around a bonfire. Kate's ears picked up the changing of the drumming cadence.

"The drums are now telling everyone to gather," said Eskadi. "Soon the story telling will begin."

Eskadi held Kate's hand as they walked among the stragglers making their way to the gathering. As they drew closer, the modulation of the drumming rose up with the suddenness of a desert wind. Just as quickly it dropped off into a dull, flat roar. The murmuring crowd that had gathered responded with a collective quietude. Little children sat peacefully on grandmothers' laps. Old men exhaled lazy swirls of smoke from their cigarettes. Teenage couples melded into each other's bodies. Kate didn't see Sheriff Hanks sitting near Song Bird's extended family.

Fry bread and soda pop were served as snacks. No one was drinking alcohol. It was strictly forbidden. Kate smiled at the older people who seemed to be curious about her.

"People are noticing you," said Eskadi. "You are going to be the subject of more than a little gossip tonight."

"I see that."

"Don't worry about it. A lot of people are looking because they wonder why I don't have a wife yet. They have been trying to get me married off ever since I came back from college. They figure I should set an example as a community leader and start having lots of children."

"What do you think of that?"

"They mean well. But…they should mind their own business," laughed Eskadi, squeezing her hand. "Come on. Let's sit down."

The pounding on the animal skinheads of the esadadedne began anew in yet another timbre. This time the tempo brought utter stillness to the crowd. The brightly painted Medicine Man, dressed in a multi-colored kilt and wearing a tall, wooden-slat headdress, danced with deliberation. Flames from the bonfire shot up behind him. Hypnotized by the events, Kate felt adrift from her usual emotions. Her mind, however, remained crystal clear as Song Bird began his story. The backdrop of the crackling fire enhanced the aura of ritual.

"The ancient spirits have spoken to me about Dzil Nchaa Si An."

The words echoed in Kate's ear. Eskadi had taught her Dzil Nchaa Si An was the Apache name for Mount Graham.

"There are many people who do not know the mountain is alive. There are many people, even among us here tonight, who think Dzil Nchaa Si An is nothing more than a big pile of stones and dirt. Many of our children and young people have never heard our sacred traditions. Some of them don't even know the creation story."

As he made this strong proclamation, from the youngest child to the eldest member, not a soul moved a single muscle. Sheriff Hanks tuned in to Song Bird's every word.

"There are Apache brothers and sisters who no longer believe the Ga'an exist anywhere but in the minds of old men who spend their days sitting around telling stories. But listen to me, the mountain spirits have come down from high atop Mount Graham. They are with us right now."

The elder males grunted like bulls. The elder women made high-pitched ululations in the back of their throats. The young children mimicked perfectly what they had just heard.

"Dzil Nchaa Si An brings us rain so that our crops may grow. How many of you have not looked upon the peaks of the mountain and seen that the Gods are going to bless us with water? When we pray in the right way, the Gods send us dark clouds, bursting full of water so the rivers may be full, the fish may grow and the crops return for another season. If we forget to pray, all of those blessings may go away and the cycle of life may cease to be."

Upon hearing the ominous warning the crowd became still.

"Many of you have lived long enough to see what happens when we forget about the proper way of living. We must teach our children how to speak to the spirits. We must, each and every one of us, remember to be thankful in our prayers when Dzil Nchaa Si Na has blessed us. To be inattentive of the mountain spirits is to be disrespectful to the Makers of the mountain. To be defiant of the Gods who bring us these precious gifts can only mean trouble."

Each spoken word appeared to penetrate young and old alike. Even teenagers were paying close attention. Zeb observed it all with a keen eye.

"The Gods have warned me that there are those who pray very hard that no rain clouds ever pass over the high peaks of Dzil Nchaa Si An."

A discernible murmur rose among the crowd as the Medicine Man spoke the dire admonition. Kate watched babies become agitated as the old women who held them began to rock and sway. Men's faces became taut and their eyes narrowed.

"It is the duty of every Apache to pray so we may continue to have the water we need. These same people who want no rain from the mountain and no clouds in the sky believe that the Ga'an spirits are nothing but dreams in the feeble minds of stupid Apaches."

Song Bird paused. The level of anxiety in the crowd rose. He held his silence until the tension was as tight as a bowstring.

"We Apaches know the Ga'an are like the wind. No one sees the wind, but who denies its existence? Who among you has not felt the gentle caress of a soft wind rolling across your skin? Is there anyone who has not heard the wind howl like a coyote mother looking for her straying child? Do we all not smell the aroma of the spring flowers drifting on the wind? Have you not tasted the dryness of the wind as it sears your mouth on a hot summer day? Who among us would be so foolish as to not respect the wind? We would be crazy not to believe in the power of the wind."

Each person in the crowd was alert now, thinking almost palpably. Each question made fundamental sense to Zeb. But what was Song Bird really saying? Zeb's skin rippled with goose flesh at Song Bird's next words. He knew something big was up, but what that thing was he could not determine. Across the way he caught the eye of Jake Dablo. The men exchanged a glance. The eye contact told him Jake was sensing something as well.

"Those very same enemies who would wish an end to the Apache Nation say that we are fools to believe in the Ga'an who have given us the ability to see and to know the power of the wind."

The hollow drums began to beat anew in subdued tones. Occasionally an accented crescendo seemed to pierce Kate's heart. The drummers muffled the sound by resting a hand atop the drum skin. The rhythmic pulsation continued for five minutes before stopping in a reverberating echo. All the while Song Bird slowly walked in a clockwise circle around the fire. Holding a string of black beads in his hand he faced the east and bowed his head in prayer. Moving to the south he repeated the same movements. This time he held a string of blue beads. Twice more he repeated the ritual. While facing the west he held yellow beads as he chanted his prayers. Caressing white beads he chanted his prayers to the north direction. Returning to his point of origin, Song Bird flourished a hidden sword from beneath his kilt. Using both hands he raised it to the sky with an offertory chant. The crowd froze at this action.

"The Ga'an on Dzil Nchaa Si An have given me a vision."

The Medicine Man lowered the sword to the center of his body. There he held it for a long minute before carefully placing it on the ground. Kneeling, the Medicine Man lit an offering of tobacco.

"The Ga'an have told me our healing plants, our curing waters, our sacred animals, our ancient burial grounds must be protected."

Song Bird picked up a handful of the earth. He turned sideways, backlit by the fire. The sand falling from his hands glistened and sparkled as it returned to the earth exactly from where the Medicine Man had snatched it. The lighter flecks of dirt were blown toward the crowd by a blast of heat from the fire. The effect of the heat on the dust particles swept them in a gyrating motion heavenward.

"My vision tells me that a small mountain will grow on top of the Great Sacred Mountain. Only it will not be made of ancient rock. The little mountain will glisten like the afternoon sunshine reflecting on water. It will be made of iron. Though it has no heartbeat, it sees through eyes made of diamonds. These precious jewels will allow it to see more clearly than a thousand eagles' eyes. The small man-made mountain of iron and steel will have the power to see right through the holes in the sky."

The tribe, nearly unable to grasp such a disparate concept, was captured between awe and disbelief as the Medicine Man ceased his homily with a final admonition.

"Each one of you will recognize it by its distinct marking. Towering above the small mountain will be a cross made of wood."

Zeb couldn't help but sense the wonder of the crowd. He, himself, felt it. But Zeb had no idea what it meant. Song Bird squatted. Taking the sword into his arms, he began dancing around the fire. One by one the adult males joined him. Mesmerized, Kate observed the lithe motions of the men as they danced in unison. When all of the men had entered the circle, the rhythm of the drumming altered, increasing dramatically in momentum. The change in the music inspired the women to begin another ululating chant. Within moments the young boys joined the men in dance and girls joined the women in wildly harmonic intonations.

Kate's eyes followed the motion of the dancers and singers. Then through the flames of the fire she noticed the few people who were not participating in the event. Jake Dablo stood stoically next to a short man with thick glasses.

The strange, beautiful noises, synchronized with the dancing movements, carried Kate into a state of ecstasy. The lightness of the night air made Kate feel she was experiencing the ancient, collective memory of the people surrounding her. From the throng emerged a smiling, young Apache child with green eyes. With a tiny hand she reached out for Kate. Silently, the child led her to the group of chanting women who welcomed her with their smiling eyes. Standing at the center of all the women was the hundred year-old Beulah Trees. Within moments Kate found herself singing the same haunting, resonating tones as the Apache women. Losing her sense of self to a sense of timelessness, she found herself staring into the glowing embers of the dying bonfire. The women and girls of the tribe hovered around her. They each touched Kate as they departed one by one. In her heightened state of awareness, she had all but forgotten about Eskadi, who was now standing by her side. Zeb and Jake had watched the entire transformation. The altered state of consciousness Kate was experiencing was not lost on them.

"Come with me."

Eskadi held her hand as they made their way to an open field. Magically, he pulled a blanket from a hiding spot and laid it on the desert ground. The world seemed perfect. Kate sat in front of Eskadi leaning against his chest. His muscular arms surrounded her. Together they gazed toward the brightly shining stars.

"Tell me, Kate, are you beginning to see what it means to be an Apache?"

"Something inside of me changed tonight. I saw things in a completely new light. It was beautiful and scary. The women were wonderful, but Song Bird's vision was scary and sometimes incomprehensible."

"Which part?"

"I understood him to be warning us about something which hasn't occurred yet. But then he spoke about it like it has already happened."

"You are right."

"How can I be right when I don't even understand what I am saying?"

"Do you remember what Song Bird said about the wind? About how it is there even though we don't see it?"

"Yes, of course."

"I think he was talking about the same thing. I think he was saying the seeds of the small mountain that will grow on top of Mount Graham have already been sewn."

"I still don't understand what it means."

"A seed that is planted can grow into a flower. Another type of seed becomes an idea. Yet another seed becomes new life. Growth of all these things occurs long before it is seen with our eyes. Song Bird was saying the seeds of the small mountain have already been planted. He knows this because a Medicine Man can perceive with his heart long before we can see with our eyes."

"How can a mountain begin to grow without anyone seeing it?"

"Song Bird said if we pray we will find the answers."

Kate, warmed by the heat of Eskadi's body, stared up at the night sky.

"While Song Bird was speaking tonight, I remembered something my dad told me when I was very young," said Kate.

"What was that?"

"When I was little, he told me the stars were holes in the sky put there by the Gods so they could peek down on the people and animals. The holes allowed the Gods to keep an eye on their creations," explained Kate.

"My father told me the same story," said Eskadi. "He told me it was a good thing because it also meant that someone would always be watching over me."

"Somebody was watching over me tonight. I

felt it."

"You mean with you and the women?" asked Eskadi.

"Yes."

"It looked to me as though they were welcoming you home."

"It feels like home."

"Then you should have an Apache name," whispered Eskadi.

A comet danced across the silent sky.

"Son-ee-ah-ray. I will call you Son-ee-ah-ray."

Eskadi ran his hands through her soft hair and hummed softly as the two of them watched the heavens through a single pair of eyes.

"Morning Star is your Apache name."

Kate was home. Her heart knew it.

CHAPTER ELEVEN

Jake sauntered through the front door of the Town Talk just in time to witness Sheriff Hanks pouring coffee for a couple of regulars.

"Hey, Zeb. If the law business doesn't work out, I'd lay some pretty good odds on Doreen turnin' you into a first class waiter. I've always said what this town needs, even more than a good sheriff, is a top notch waiter."

"You're a real hoot, Jake, a real barrel of laughs. Now have a seat before your flapping lips cool down this pot of java."

"Make mine hot and blacker than midnight on a new moon. As to my jive, well hell, go ahead and shoot me for being happy. I happen to be feeling extra special good today."

Zeb set the coffee pot down. He gave Jake the once over. This amount of joviality could mean only one of two things. Either Jake was thinking about stargazing, his passion, or crime solving, his true gift.

"Every time you start acting like a young man instead of an older one, I get to feeling something is about to bust loose. Am I right or am I right?"

Before Jake could answer, Doreen Nightingale came swooping down on the men like a hungry hawk on a floundering field mouse.

"If it ain't the best dang lookin' men in the southern half of the state of Arizona. Yes siree, two handsome fellers that make it easy on a gal's eyes. You gentlemen are cuter than little boys could ever hope to be," exclaimed Doreen, tousling Jake's hair and kissing the top of Zeb's head.

"Good afternoon, Doe," said Jake. 'Your boyfriend here has been sassing on me. Now I wonder where he learned that kind of back talk?"

"Don't look at me, bright eyes. Maybe he's got a little crush on ya'? He has been actin' a little on the romantic side lately, if ya' know what I mean."

Doreen tossed a wink and a smile at the retired sheriff.

"Doreen, quit your teasing. People might get the wrong idea overhearing something like that," pleaded Zeb.

Doreen reached over and planted a kiss with a loud smack on her boyfriend's cheek.

"Hell, let 'em talk. Now can I get you girls somethin' or are you just in here for coffee klatch?"

"Doreen!"

"Oh, shush. If anyone asks, I'll swear on a stack of Bibles that I got first-hand knowledge that you ain't no Nancy boy. Now, what'll it be, ladies?"

"The coffee's good enough for me."

"I'll take a couple of sugared doughnuts to go with my cup of joe," said Jake.

"Comin' right up."

Doreen sashayed to the counter for the sweets.

"Zeb, you busy today?" asked Jake.

"Not overly. Mostly routine. Why?"

"Got a few extra hours you can spare?"

"Maybe. Depends on what you have in mind?"

"I spent yesterday at the courthouse looking up some plat marks. I found the exact location of the land the Catholic Church and its partners are looking to take over up on top of Mount Graham."

"This is about that planning commission meeting you dragged me to, isn't it? AIMGO? That was the corporation, wasn't it?"

"Yup and yup"

"I might have guessed."

"Now just hear me out."

"As I'm still working on my first cup of coffee, I don't know if I have any choice in the matter."

"I plotted it out on a map, but bear in mind that I'm no cartographer."

"No what?"

"Cartographer. A map maker. I think I've got that parcel of land pinpointed."

"So? It's land, it's on the mountain. What difference does it make other than Farrell's got his undies in a bunch about it?"

"Depending on precisely where it is it might make a significant difference to a lot of people."

"How so?"

"If I'm right, and I'm damn near certain I am, and if the Catholic Church and the AIMGO Corporation end up with that property, you are going to have one hell of a mess on your hands."

"That is a lot of ifs and ands."

"Didn't say I knew for certain."

"Okay. What kind of a mess?"

"Listen up and you'll find out. After I looked up the location from the maps down at the courthouse, I visited with Song Bird."

"Would you quit beating around the bush and start making sense?"

"The reason I went out and had a little chat with Song Bird is because he and I have spent a night or two together up on top of Mount Graham. I taught him about looking at the constellations through the telescope and shared the stories my grandfather taught me with him. Song Bird taught me the Apache legends and myths related to the mountain spirits. The first time we went up there, Song Bird and I looked at the stars from this secret spot my grandfather showed me years ago. Second time we went up there together we went back to the very same place."

Over the years Zeb had listened to Jake's stories so many times he could tell them as his own. But this was a tale he was not familiar with.

"Then some time passed, maybe five or six years, maybe more, before Song Bird and I went back up there together. During that time we got to know each other real well. We came to trust each other in a way most people never do, much less an Apache and a White law man. We went back up there again, a third time to the same spot. When I took the telescope out, Song Bird stopped me. He said we should go to another place. He called it an ancient place. We walked a short distance, and this is going to sound crazy, but it felt like we were at the highest point on the whole planet. It's like we were only one step away from a gateway to another world, maybe even heaven."

Jake closed his eyes as he unfolded the story. Zeb listened so as not to miss a word.

"Song Bird told me it was the most sacred spot on the mountain. I'm telling you, never before or since have I seen the sky with such perfection. I felt as though I were floating through space right up to heaven."

"That's a fine story, Jake, but something about it doesn't make sense. Why would Song Bird show that place to you? Sacred Apache spots aren't for White people."

"You're right. That's normally true. I had the same question. I asked Song Bird why he was showing it to me."

"And?"

"He acted mysterious and answered me in a riddle. He said I already knew the answer. He said that answer would be revealed to me when the time was right."

"Do you think the time is now?" asked Zeb.

"Yes, I do. I think the sacred spot Song Bird showed me is the land the Catholic Church and AIMGO own," said Jake.

"Well, if the Church owns it, there isn't a lot anyone can do, is there? I mean legally that is."

Jake leaned forward and stared into Zeb's eyes. The look he gave him brought an instant chill to

Zeb and prickled the hair on his neck.

"You know this to be true, Zeb. Some things are outside the law."

Zeb's mind went directly to Red Parrish and Red Junior.

"Jesus, Jake. Keep your voice down. Listen to what you're saying. If people hear you talking, I am gonna have big trouble."

"I know exactly what I'm saying. Remember when you, me and Song Bird sat out at his place around the campfire, and he was telling us Apache legends of Geronimo and Cochise."

"Well, hell yes, of course. How could I forget a night like that? He taught me more Apache history in one night than I've learned in the rest of my life."

"Remember when he was telling us there were only a few things that would make the Apaches declare out and out war on the United States again?"

"I remember thinking he was crazy when he said it. I mean the very idea of a tribe attacking the United States of America."

"One thing that would get the entire Apache Nation united and riled up to do something that drastic would be someone trying to take away their Holy Place on Mount Graham," said Jake.

"You're right. That's exactly what he said."

"I think the Catholic Church and the AIMGO Corporation have got designs on doing precisely that. If they get away with it, we're all going to have one hell of a mess on our hands."

"You may have a hell of a mess on your hands, but it ain't gonna be as much a one as these gooey pastries I make," said Doreen as she interrupted their conversation by placing a plateful of freshly baked goods in front of the men. "Now what the heck is this? Some kind of map?"

Doreen reached to the floor and picked up a piece of folded paper.

"Official United States Forest Service Topographic Map of Mount Graham. Well, I'll be a monkey's aunt."

"Here, that's mine," garbled Jake through a mouthful of jelly donut. "It must have fallen out of my pocket."

"Now ain't that what you'd call a major league coincidence?"

The men munched on the fresh goodies. Doreen opened up the map and spread it out on the table.

"I'm not much of one for readin' maps. I can look at a road map okay to get where I'm goin', but these here fancy maps, I hardly ever waste time lookin' at the dang things. And then, whadda' ya' know? Just like that, twice in one day I bend over and pick up an official forest service map of Mount Graham. Right here in the Town Talk. Now don't that beat all?"

Jake and Zeb exchanged clueless glances.

"You two look dumber than a pair of jackasses in a stare down contest at a county fair."

"What are you talking about, Doe?" asked Zeb.

"Why, just this mornin' in the front corner booth over by the window someone plumb left a briefcase behind. Now right away you'd think I woulda' known whose it was. After all, how many people carry around a briefcase? Huh?"

Doreen paused, waiting for an answer.

"Not many," answered Zeb.

"That's right, honey. Dang few folks around these parts got the need. Just a couple of lawyers and maybe a real estate agent or two. So I went backwards in my mind to see who sat in that booth this morning. I came up blank. Nobody sat there this morning. So I got to thinkin'. The whole thing seemed like it was right out of a spy movie. Like a Matt Helm flick or somethin'. Didn't you just love Dean Martin in those movies?"

"Sure did," said Jake.

"Me, too," said Doreen. "So I got to askin' myself, did someone plant it there for someone else to find? Maybe inside was diamonds or gold or money. Maybe even secret plans."

"I think you may be watching too many spy movies, Doe," said Zeb.

"Hush up, handsome. If I could make up stories that easy in my head, well, I'd have a full time job at the Inquirer or in Hollywood. So back to what I was sayin' to begin with before old bright eyes here started yappin'. I thought back to last night and sure enough I figured out right away whose it was. Zeb, you remember that little skinny doctor with the girly hands that we ran into up on the Mount?"

"Dr. Bede?"

"Yeah, that's the guy."

"I guess we all know him," added Jake.

"That's right. You met him at the county planning commission meeting."

"I ran into him out at the San Carlos, too," added Jake. "He came out to hear Song Bird's story of Mount Graham."

"You two ladies gonna' quit your gossipin' and let me finish my story?"

"Sorry, Doe, go on."

"Anyway, just to make sure it wasn't a spy's briefcase I opened it up to see if I could find some ID. You know, so I could return it to its rightful owner. Well, soon as I open it up, a map of Mount Graham, just like the one you got there, Jake, falls out onto the floor."

"I suppose you searched the spy case thoroughly?" asked Zeb.

"Sugar plum, I hope you don't think I'm the kind of gal who snoops through other people's personal belongins? I know you think better of me than that. Besides, I didn't have to dig too deep. Right there was a letter addressed to Dr. Venerable Bede. That was that. I didn't need to look no further. Then I remembered he was sittin' in that front booth all by his lonesome. I felt sorry for the little guy, so I gave him a piece of homemade apple pie on the house. Now I just gotta wait for him to come back in and pick up the briefcase."

"Wait no longer," said Jake. "You're looking at Dr. Bede's personal delivery service. It just so happens Zeb and I are headed up that way right now."

"I suppose if I can't trust a couple of lawmen with the goods, who can I trust? Let me run and grab it for you. You sure you two ain't headed up to Riggs Lake to do some fishin', now are ya'?"

"No, Doreen, its official business," assured Jake.

The sheriff shot an inquisitive leer in the former sheriff's direction.

"Well, let me put it differently," said Jake. "It might become official business."

Zeb finished his coffee, leaving his usual oversized gratuity for Doreen. Jake grabbed a donut for the road. Within minutes the men were heading west on Route 366. As they passed the Graham County Market, three old men sitting on the porch waved. Jake returned their salute.

"Doc Yackley gave me all the details about the death of Father McNamara."

"There were hardly any secrets there," replied Zeb, "just a very dramatic and strange case of suicide."

"I mean about the ring he was wearing."

"All priests wear a church ring. It's part of the Roman Catholic thing. It shows what Order they belong to. Why, what did Doc say about the ring?"

"Not much. He just described it to me," replied Jake.

"What are you getting at, Jake?"

"Nothing really. Just a feeling I've got."

"Let's hear it. I know you're itching to say something."

"My grandpa used to say, 'If you got an itch, scratch it cause it's your insides trying to speak out.' I think about that little adage every time I get a notion."

"What are you thinking, Jake? Damn, I never heard you hedge a bet so much in all the years I've known you."

"It's not that I'm being evasive. Both you and I know just how easy it is when you beat around the bush to scare up something other than what you're looking for. I'm trying to avoid just that."

"Spit it out, Jake."

"Just set back for a second and put this together in your head. One, a dead Catholic priest wearing a ring with some writing about the Vatican Astronomical Observatory on it. Two, mix that in with this business about the Catholic Church quietly buying up a lot of property up on the mountain, maybe the best star gazing spot on damn near the whole planet. Put one and one together and you might just have something."

"You might have what?"

"Now hold your horses. Then you throw in the fact the Apaches would practically be willing to go to war over the spot because it's sacred and…"

"There's more? I'm not so sure I want to hear anything else!"

"John Farrell, using the planning commission and his real estate office, just may have a little dirt on his hands. It just seems like too many forces coming together all at once to mean anything except trouble brewing on the horizon."

"Damn it, Jake, you know full good and well from all your years as sheriff it could be nothing more than coincidence, too. It's a big damn world out there. There's always all sorts of shit happening."

Jake looked straight ahead through the car window. In the distance below, snuggled against the desert floor, sat the city of Safford. Jake once again drummed his fingers against the top of the steering wheel. He spoke so quietly Zeb strained his ears to hear.

"But it isn't, Zeb. It's no coincidence. And, I can see that you feel it too."

CHAPTER TWELVE

Zeb watched his reflection roll across the car windshield with each switchback on the twisted, winding road that led to the Riggs Lake campground atop Mount Graham. The crow's feet at the corners of his eyes seemed more sharply defined than ever. There was no denying his job was taking a physical toll on his body. A single glance toward Jake warned him precisely how the law business could consume a man if he wasn't careful.

"Pull in over there so we can return the briefcase to Dr. Bede."

Zeb parked in the small lot. It was vacant except for Bede's truck.

"Doesn't look like he's around," said Zeb.

"Maybe he's out doing some field work."

"Halloo...Doctor Bede," shouted the sheriff.

An echo from a nearby canyon returned his call.

"Doesn't look like he's within earshot," said Zeb.

"Let's take a hike. We're not too far from where we wanted to go anyway."

Jake pulled the map out of his pocket and carefully unfolded it on top of a large boulder. Removing his glasses from a case, he placed them on his head. They immediately slipped to the tip of his nose.

"Here's the lake."

Jake tapped a weathered finger against the map as he squinted through his bifocals, measuring his bearings. He looked up at the lake then back down at the map several times. Sliding a rough hand smoothly across the plat to a second point, he tapped again.

"And here's where we want to be."

Zeb leaned on the rock and eyeballed the map.

"How the hell are we going to know exactly where we are? I mean there aren't markings up here. We could be off the mark by a quarter of a mile or more. How would we ever know? We're on some sort of wild goose chase if you ask me."

"Normally, I'd say you'd be right, but I did a little homework. The records filed at the courthouse indicate a private survey crew, out of Phoenix, came up here and marked the corner boundaries of the AIMGO property with orange flags. I talked with Ed Johnson over at the county survey office. He said the flags should be mounted on poles with numbers written on them."

"And when we find them, then what?"

"Then we know where they are," replied Jake.

"Exactly what good will that be to us?"

"I'm not exactly sure."

"Damn it, Jake, you're starting to give me a headache."

"Zeb, you're just going to have to trust my gut on this one."

The sheriff followed Jake through the spruce

trees for half a mile. The foliage gave way abruptly, revealing a magnificent sky. Jake smiled as he watched Zeb staring spellbound toward the sky.

"What do you think, Zeb?"

"You weren't kidding. This is weird. It's almost like you can reach up and touch the sky."

"I know. This is the spot that both my grandfather and Song Bird showed me. This is a holy place for the Apaches, maybe even their most sacred spot." Jake's voice was both low and humble.

"Is it okay for us to be here?"

"Yes. Both my grandfather and Song Bird showed me this place for a reason. Something in my heart told me it was important for you to see and feel this place."

Zeb walked toward the horizon. His arms felt weighty. He struggled to lift them from his side. Each advancing step increased his sluggishness until he felt as though he was wading through a sea of mud. Previously unheard sounds reverberated in his ears. Nearly paralyzed by his strange surroundings, Zeb began gasping for air when a hand grasped his shoulder.

"We should leave. Now!" commanded Jake.

With an unsteady gait Zeb followed Jake off the peak, away from the sacred spot.

"What happened to me?" begged Zeb.

"I don't know. I just know it is a very powerful place."

The trail widened and the surroundings became familiar again. By the time the men neared the Riggs Lake campground, Zeb felt normal.

"There's our man," said Jake.

Dr. Bede rose to greet them from a lawn chair he had placed at the edge of the lake.

"Hello, Sheriff Hanks, Mr. Dablo. I saw the police car and I figured it was you. What brings you two way up here today?"

"Actually, it's you, Dr. Bede, that we have come to see," replied Sheriff Hanks.

"Have...have I done something wrong? Was I supposed to get an extension on my camping permit?"

"No," laughed Zeb. "We're returning something that belongs to you."

"My briefcase? I get so absent-minded. I must have forgotten it in town. Let me see. Was it at the library or the courthouse?"

"You left it at the Town Talk last night."

"Oh, yes. That cozy little restaurant with the loud waitress."

"Better watch what you say or you might get arrested," said Jake.

"What did I say? I don't want to get arrested."

"You just insulted the sheriff's girlfriend. That's what."

"Oh, I'm sorry. I should have recognized her. She's the woman that was up here with you that night? Right?"

"That's right. Not too many people forget

Doreen so easily."

"I am sorry. It's not that she's so loud, but I spend most of my time alone and in nature. When someone bellows out their words, I mean when someone speaks loudly, well, I have sensitive ears. I'm sorry. I meant no insult to her."

"Forget about it," said the sheriff, shrugging his shoulders.

"Pardon my bad manners. Would you men care for some coffee? It will only take a minute to heat some up. I already have some made. I can heat it on my Coleman."

"Sure, why not?" replied Jake.

"I could use a cup of coffee myself," added Zeb.

"You know it's very nice to have some company," began Dr. Bede, lighting the burner on the stove. "I spend a lot of time up here by myself. To be honest, it can get sort of lonely."

"How long have you been on this project anyway?" asked Zeb.

"Six weeks now. Three weeks of preparation time at my office. Three weeks, as of today, up here in the field, as we call it. The forest service has extensive rules and regulatory requirements I have to follow. You know how bureaucrats are."

Jake and Zeb nodded. Both knew a man's job was as much dotting the i's and crossing the t's as it was actually doing the work. Bede may have been a highly educated doctor doing scientific fieldwork, but he was still beholden to higher ups.

"Since you're the expert, what makes Mount

MARK REPS

Graham so unique?" asked Jake.

"This mountain isn't like any other in the entire United States. It has five distinct ecological zones."

"No kidding," said Jake. "I guess living around it you just take it for granted.

"That's natural. Most people take for granted what they expect they'll always have," said Bede.

"Now you said there are five zones. What does that mean?" asked Jake.

"Down by the base of the mountain it is desert flora with cactus and all the scrub undergrowth indicative of the area. Coming up the mountain next is the Pinion/Juniper belt, followed by the Pine/Oak belt, the Fir/Aspen belt and, at the top of the mountain, the Spruce/Fir belt with its old growth forest."

"So what does the Forest Service want from this?"

"Their particular interest, as far as my project is concerned, lies in the old growth forest near the top of the mountain."

"What does the wife think of you being gone all the time?" asked Jake.

"Oh heavens, I'm not married. I'm afraid I have no time for that sort of thing."

As Bede poured the men their coffee, a horn honked in the background. The men turned to see Deputy Delbert.

"Good, more company," said Bede.

"Damn," said Zeb. "I forgot Delbert had rural

136

patrol up here today. I could have saved him the drive."

"Howdy Jake, Sheriff," said Delbert. "You guys fishin'?"

Zeb explained the reason for their visit and introduced the deputy to Bede.

"You men aren't interested in a little dinner are you?" asked Bede. "I picked up a six pack of beer last time I was in town. I could make us all something to eat."

The loneliness in his voice allowed only one answer.

"Hell, yes," said Jake.

"Sounds okay," said Zeb.

"I am awful hungry," added Delbert.

"Great. I bought some fresh hamburger. A beer would go nicely with that."

"None for me," said Jake. "You're looking at a teetotaler."

"I'll have one," said Delbert

"Ditto," said Zeb.

"Coming right up."

Doctor Bede sprinted over to his tent, opened the flap and ran back, beers in hand.

"I couldn't help but notice your telescope over there," said Jake.

"It's a little hobby of mine, astronomy that is," replied Doctor Bede. "With all the time I spend in these high elevations, it helps pass the time."

"It's a hobby of mine, too. My grandfather taught me."

"Really? What a coincidence, so did mine," replied the doctor.

"Do you have a favorite constellation?" asked Jake.

"As a matter of fact I do. It's Perseus, because of Algol."

"The Demon's Head. I know it well. The ancient Hebrews thought it resembled the Devil's head."

"A wonderful bit of superstition," said Bede. "An unexplained dimming of a star to the ancients who knew nothing of eclipsing binary stars would certainly be disturbing. Wouldn't you agree?"

"Of course. That is why all the old maps depict it as the eye of the severed head of Medusa."

"I commend your knowledge. How about yourself? What group of stars is your favorite?"

"Orion," replied Jake. "Because of Rigel."

"Of course," said the doctor thoughtfully. "Who wouldn't love a bright double star that represents beauty and enlightenment?"

The unique kinship of a shared passion stirred something inside of Jake to share the story of the tragic death of his granddaughter, Rigella. But Bede spoke first.

"The eyes of a vengeful but watchful God see through beautiful Rigel."

"What? What did you say?" asked Jake.

"Rigel," replied the doctor. "The ancient Syrians, long before the Greeks and the Romans, believed in the power of that star."

"I don't know the story told by the Syrians."

"You know the Greek mythological story?"

"Yes," replied Jake. "Orion, the handsome and beautiful hunter, was the lover of Diana. When she accidentally killed him, she placed him in the heavens to be near her. It's near Taurus in the sky. Rigel and Betelgeuse are stars in Orion."

"Very good. You know your stars very well. I'm surprised you haven't heard of the ancient myth of Rigel."

"Please tell me," begged Jake.

"The ancient ones believed the Creator looked down upon the world from behind the stars. They believed he could see everything going on. So as not to surprise and scare the people, the Creator disguised his eyes as bright stars. The twin stars in Rigel were believed to be the eyes of God."

"You said a watchful and vengeful god."

"In the ancient times when people were at the whim of nature, much more so than we are today, they prayed to God to watch over them. In like manner and knowing that nature must unleash its fury, they prayed God send His vengeance upon their enemies."

Jake was visibly overcome with melancholy. The horrible vengeance entangled in his granddaughter's death was retribution directed at him but taken out on her. Why had God forsaken his granddaughter? Why had God forsaken him? Where were the eyes of God then?

"Jake? Jake? Are you okay?" Delbert's normal,

reassuring voice snapped Jake from his bitter remembrance.

"Did I say something wrong?" asked an apologetic Doctor Bede.

"No. It was nothing," replied Jake.

"Well, I guess if I'm going to have dinner guests, I'd better get to work," said Bede.

"Anything I can do to help?" asked Deputy Delbert.

"Sure. You can get me my supply sack."

Bede pointed to a knapsack tied to a tree branch above the reach of bears and other wild animals.

"Mind if I grab myself another beer while I'm at it?" asked Delbert.

"Wait, I'll get it for you," said Bede, scrambling to his feet.

"Don't bother. I can get it."

Opening the tent flap and reaching for the cooler, Delbert did an involuntary double take. Inside of the tent was an altar enshrined with an icon of Christ on the Cross, a statue of the Blessed Virgin Mary, a rosary and a Bible. Lying next to the Bible were the neatly folded vestments of a priest. To the side of the clothing a small sign written in blood red ink read, 'The Sacred Heart of Jesus Forgives the Sins of All Men'.

Delbert reached into the cooler. Next to the beer were four liquid filled vials. Delbert pulled his head out of the tent, acting as if he had seen nothing out of the ordinary.

"I see you found one," said Bede, moving to

position himself between the deputy and the tent.

"Yah, I got a cold one. Thanks," said Delbert, hoisting his beer to the doctor.

After dinner Bede invited the men to have a look through his telescope.

"No thanks, not tonight. Maybe some other time," replied Jake. "It's time we hit the road."

"I'd be delighted if sometime you would come back and share my looking glass with me."

"Some other time, perhaps," said Jake.

The men thanked Bede and headed down the mountain. In the car Jake made little attempt at conversation. Zeb gave some small talk a shot.

"The little guy can cook pretty darn good, wouldn't you say?"

"Yup, I guess," replied Jake. "Couldn't help but notice you bypassed the parsnips."

"They don't do much for me," replied Zeb.

"Me neither, I didn't eat any, but I saw Delbert take a small bite of one. He chewed the parsnips for a few seconds. Maybe even swallowed a bit of 'em. But then he spit the rest of it out like he'd bitten into a rotten tomato."

As wordless minutes passed, Zeb observed Jake staring sullenly out the window.

"Jake, you're too quiet for your own good. What's on your mind?"

"I was just thinking about my granddaughter."

Zeb nodded. Innocent Rigella had been murdered by a vengeful son who was seeking a pound of flesh from the former sheriff as retribution for the death of his own father. Jake's obsession with finding the killer cost him his career, his wife and nearly his will to live. The pain of a broken heart and the knowledge he would grow old without having grandchildren to teach about the stars weighed heavily on the injured soul of the ex-sheriff.

The men drove in silence as the big yellow moon shining on the desert floor created an eerie luminescence throughout the valley.

CHAPTER THIRTEEN

Jake rose early and headed to the Town Talk for coffee and eggs. He was surprised to see the early morning regulars congregating near the front door of the diner.

"Don't tell me Doreen is locking people out of her business these days?"

A toothless old man puffing on a hand rolled cigarette growled out an answer.

"Locked up tighter than a drum. Dark as night in there."

Another elderly gentleman, holding his hands on the sides of his head, pushed his face against the windowpane in a vain attempt to see something that wasn't there.

"If she was out carousin' all night, I only wish I had been her escort," he joked.

His words were received with a round of gritty laughter.

Jake looked up and down the street. Doreen's car was nowhere to be seen. The town hall clock read five twenty and she always opened at five sharp.

"I'll go wake her up," offered Jake.

The waiting men nodded in agreement to the idea as Jake climbed behind the wheel of his truck and drove the few short blocks to her house. Jake pulled around the back of the house to see if Doreen's car was parked in the alley. It was.

When no one answered his knock, Jake let himself in through the unlocked door.

"Hello. Anybody home? Doreen? Zeb?"

Jake left the empty house with an uneasy feeling. Even though a tough decade had passed since he last wore a badge, instinct took over. He drove directly to the hospital. The sheriff's truck was parked near the emergency room door. Inside, the duty nurse, Jill Jerome, was busy filling out intake forms.

"Jill, are Doreen Nightingale and Sheriff Hanks in the emergency room?"

"Good morning to you, too," replied the nurse.

"Sorry, Jill. Good morning," said Jake.

"As to your question, yes, Doreen Nightingale is, and so is the sheriff."

"Did something happen to Doreen?"

"No," said the nurse.

"Is the sheriff okay?"

"He's fine."

"Then what are they doing here?"

"I can't say. Patient confidentiality."

"Come on, Jill. It's me, Jake. For criminy sakes."

Jill Jerome, R.N., was tired and a touch crabby at the end of a busy night shift. She was in no mood for an argument. She glanced around the waiting room one more time to make sure no one overheard her. She whispered to Jake.

"Deputy Delbert Funke is in there. He came in last night. We pumped his stomach."

"Why? What for?"

"It looks like food poisoning."

"What? Food poisoning?"

"Zeb and I ate the same food he ate last night and we're not sick," said Jake.

"Maybe he had an early breakfast," said the nurse. "I'm sure he'll tell you when he feels like talking."

Jake grabbed a cup of coffee and took a seat. A few minutes later Doreen came walking down the hallway.

"What in the hell is going on, Doreen?"

"It's Delbert. He's sicker than the puppy that ate grandpa's slippers."

"Here, have a seat," offered Jake. "Tell me what happened."

"Last night Zeb came over to my place around ten. It was just after you guys got back from up on the Mount. He was plumb tuckered and we hit the rack early."

"Go on."

"The way I heard it, Delbert started feeling sick to his stomach on the ride down the Mount. By the time he got home he couldn't hardly get his breath. Mrs. Funke said five minutes later he was layin' on his back, eyes wide open, kinda like a deer in the headlights. Then, all of the sudden, right out of the blue, his chest started heaving up and down like a house afire. He puked up a greasy black hunk of gunk."

"Good lord."

"Then poor ol' Delbert fell to the floor and started spasmin' all over the place like he was having a fit or a whatcha' call it?"

"Seizure?"

"Yeah, a seizure. She panicked and called the sheriff's department. When the night gal couldn't get no one to answer at the ambulance place, she called my place. I guess she knows Zeb stays there once in a while these days. Zeb got the message, and we high-tailed it over there and dragged the big lug to the car. When we got down here, they had to call Doc Yackley and get him over here STAT, that means fast."

Jake walked to the nurse's station. He told Nurse Jill he knew what was going on. She still would not allow him into the room but agreed to walk back there and get an update. She returned with a somber expression on her face.

"Doc will be right out to talk with you."

Before Jake had a chance to respond, Doc Yackley and Zeb came walking down the hallway.

"Doc, I don't like the look on your face. How serious is it?"

"I thought it was acute food poisoning, but it might be something else. I'm not exactly sure what it is."

"What makes you think it's something else?" asked Jake.

"He vomited, but I pumped his stomach anyway. What came out looked like carrots, meat of some kind and some beer."

"I'm sure Zeb told you we had dinner with Delbert last night. He had some carrots, a hamburger, a couple of beers and maybe one small bite of parsnips."

"What do you mean, maybe one small bite of parsnips?" asked Doc.

"He took a bite of parsnips, chewed it a bit, then spit it out. From the look on his face you could sure tell he didn't like the taste of it."

"Did you eat the same thing?" asked the Doc, pulling a pipe from his pocket.

"Pretty much. I wasn't real hungry."

"How about the beer?"

"I haven't had a drink in a few years, Doc. I don't intend to start now."

"I had one," said Zeb.

"Was the beer home brew?"

"Nope. From a bottle. Store bought."

"Well, I'm going to watch him today. He's having some trouble breathing. I'm going to keep him in the hospital so I can keep an eye on him."

"What do you mean he's havin' some trouble breathing?" asked a distraught Doreen.

"Sometimes when people convulse like he did, their breathing apparatus goes into spasm, and it makes it difficult for them to breathe. I suspect that's what's going on with him now."

"When will you know for certain?"

"If it's food poisoning, he should be improving by this afternoon."

"And if it ain't?"

"Then we'll do some more tests. We're doing everything we can right now."

"Why don't you try and go about your normal routine. People around the Town Talk must be wondering where you are."

"Oh, my God. I plumb forgot about work," said Doreen. "Hon', can you get me over there pronto?"

"Sure thing."

"I'll call Zeb with an update. There's nothing any of you can do for him right now. He doesn't need to get excited. He needs to lie still and take it easy. That's the best way for this thing to pass," said Doc.

"Mind if I stick my nose in?" asked Jake.

"He's got some tubes in him to help him breathe. I gave him some medication to make him relax. He's almost asleep. You can go in for a minute."

Turning the corner into the hospital's emergency treatment room, Jake eyed Delbert, full of plastic tubes and hooked up to machines, barely alert.

"He looks like the swill in the bottom of a slop bucket, doesn't he, Doc? Jesus, he looks terrible."

"His fences could use some mending, that's for sure. We're going to have to give him some time."

"He's not going to die, is he, Doc?"

"I know he doesn't look his best right now."

"Take care of him, Doc. He's a good boy."

Doc Yackley lowered his voice and spoke

seriously to Jake.

"I didn't want to say this in front of Doreen. I'm going to have him taken to Tucson by ambulance if he's not improving in the next hour. I don't have any choice. He's having a heck of a time breathing. I don't have the equipment or the personnel to handle it. He needs to be watched around the clock. He'll be better off up there."

"That's not good at all, is it?" asked Jake.

"Now you understand why I didn't say anything in front of Doreen."

An hour later an unconscious Deputy Funke was loaded onto a gurney for transport to the Carondelet Neurological Institute in Tucson.

CHAPTER FOURTEEN

"Deputy Steele, you have a call on line one from Eskadi Black Robes."

The curtness of Helen Nazelrod's voice cut like a knife.

"Thank you, Helen. I'll take it in here."

The secretary's dislike of Eskadi Black Robes related to his direct order to keep Mormon missionaries off of the reservation. She considered this a slap in the face to her faith.

"Hello, Eskadi"

"Hon-dah, Son-ee-ah-ray."

Kate felt a warm flush on her face and a flutter in her heart as Eskadi greeted her by her newly acquired Apache name.

"To what do I owe the pleasure of this call?"

"I'd like to say it's a pleasure, but actually it's business. It's about Beulah Trees."

"Is she okay?"

"She's fine, but I think you're going to want to talk with her."

"What about?"

"Those foreclosure papers you served on her."

"Did you talk her into changing her mind about trying to get the land back?"

"No. I wish I could. But, on that particular issue, I must respect her wishes."

"What is it then?"

"Beulah remembered something she had forgotten to tell me. Actually, I don't know if she forgot it or just thought it wasn't important. It came to her the night Song Bird told the story of Mount Graham."

Kate felt the tingle that comes with awareness shoot up her spine. That night was also the night she first felt love in her heart for Eskadi. Kate swiveled in her chair turning toward the painting on the wall behind her desk, a gift from Eskadi long before he cast his spell upon her.

"Do you think I should talk with Beulah personally?"

"I know she trusts you. I think you can get the best information from talking with her face to face."

"Would you want to come along?"

"I was waiting for an invitation," laughed Eskadi.

"I'll be there in an hour."

The ride out to the reservation passed quickly. Kate divided her time mulling over the potential information Beulah might have and daydreaming about Eskadi.

Eskadi was standing near a mesquite tree talking to some men when she arrived. The men smiled and waved to her. One old man slapped Eskadi on the back as he headed toward her car.

"George Two Fingers and Fergus Sneezie don't understand why a woman would want to be a deputy sheriff. They think it's a man's job. You're a bit of a conundrum in their eyes."

"I trust you defended my honor."

"I told them if they thought they could do a better job than you, they should apply for the position. Mostly they think you're too pretty to be a deputy sheriff."

"I'm flattered," said Kate. "But I am also on the clock. Let's go."

The road to Beulah's house was lined with hard, deep ruts. Kate had to swerve to avoid large boulders that jutted ominously in the middle of the road every thirty or forty feet.

"What's with all these oddly placed stones? Why doesn't someone move them?"

"I asked Beulah that very question."

"And?"

"She told me I had filled my head with too much education. She said she was damn sorry she voted for such a stupid man as me to be the tribal chairman."

"Was she serious?"

"Partially. She said the Gods put them there for a reason. She scolded me for thinking that I knew how to handle something the Gods had created."

Kate looked toward Eskadi who shrugged and smiled impishly.

"Pull over by that mesquite tree and we'll walk down the trail. It's easier than driving."

A gently sloped pathway led to a run-down, tar-paper shack shaded by a dense overgrowth of trees whose lower branches scraped the ground. Beulah was sitting out front in a homemade rocking chair, fanning herself as they arrived.

Eskadi hailed her from a distance, properly waiting for the traditional permission to move on to her property.

"Hello, Mrs. Trees."

"I heard the two of you plodding down the trail. One man with hard-soled shoes. One woman walking in man's boots," remarked Beulah.

"Hello, Mrs. Trees," said Kate.

The deep crevasses in the ancient face of the old woman softened as their eyes connected.

"It always makes me happy to see the face of a young woman in love. It refreshes my energy."

Kate looked toward Eskadi who signaled with a slight shake of the head that meant he had said nothing to Beulah about the two of them.

"No one had to tell me, dearie."

Beulah peered over the top of her bifocals.

"An aura is an aura. It glows like a halo. Either you see it or you don't. It's something you cannot hide from an old lady like me. Please come into my house. We'll make some tea."

Mrs. Trees' house, furnished with little more than a bed, a chair and a few cooking utensils, spoke directly to the reservation poverty Eskadi was working to change. The only decorations were a dozen yellowing photographs thumbtacked to the wall.

"You like those pictures?" she asked.

"Yes. They're lovely," replied Kate.

"Those pictures on the left are me and my

sisters. They were taken by the first White man to come this way. I mean the first White man with a camera in his hand instead of a gun. I know that sounds shocking to a young person like you, but that's how times were. Now things are changing. Everybody comes with a camera."

Kate smiled broadly at the old woman's observation.

"You've got a good sense of humor," said Beulah. "You should teach that young man of yours it is okay to laugh. For a young feller, he is a little too much about business."

"I'll work on him, Mrs. Trees."

"The two old people in the middle, those are my parents."

Kate looked at the handsome couple who bore the sternest of looks on their faces.

"Nobody knew how to smile for a picture in those days. Getting shot by a camera was almost as serious as getting shot at by a gun."

Beulah chuckled. Her sense of humor was lost on these young love birds.

"I've heard that in the old days Indians, uh, Native Americans, were afraid that if they were photographed their spirit might get captured," said Kate.

"Don't believe everything you hear," replied Beulah. "White people will say just about anything to make the Apache people look superstitious and backwards. And, by the way, I am an Indian, an Apache. I suppose young people like to be called Native Americans."

"First Americans," added Eskadi.

Beulah hesitated for a moment. "Eskadi, you are a nice boy, nice young man, but your fire is misdirected sometimes." Her words silenced the room.

Kate eased the temporary awkwardness by pointing to a picture of a young man dressed in full Apache regalia standing next to a dappled horse.

"Who's this handsome young man?"

"It's the same man in the next picture. Here, look closer."

Kate and Eskadi leaned forward in the dimly lit shack to see a picture of the same young man wearing an old-fashioned looking military uniform.

"That is Standing Trees. He was going to be my husband. We never married."

Mrs. Trees' aged hands trembled slightly as she poured tea.

"Why didn't you marry him?"

"He went away to fight the White man's war. He never came back."

"I'm sorry."

"It's strange how life can be. Standing Trees' father was an Apache warrior who was killed in battle against the White man. Then not so many years later Standing Trees died fighting for the White man against other White men. All that fighting and dying. And what for?"

Beulah took the picture down off the wall. Softly she rubbed a wrinkled finger across the young warrior's face.

"I married him in my heart. I took his name for my own. Not once did I ever look for another man to be my husband. I had room for only one in my heart."

"That's a beautiful love story, Mrs. Trees."

"Yes it is, but you didn't come here to listen to an old woman remember the way things used to be, now did you?"

"Well, we, uh," began Eskadi.

"Oh never you mind, young man. I won't keep you any longer with my old stories. Besides, if I tell you all of them today, you might not come back to see me another day."

"Oh, we will be back to see you. You can count on that," reassured Kate.

The promise of future company brought a smile to the semi-toothless grin of Beulah Trees.

"Now, I don't want the two of you to think I'm losing my marbles…"

"We don't think that at all, Mrs. Trees."

"You can call me Beulah."

"Beulah."

An air of serenity overcame Beulah as Kate spoke her name.

"It's always refreshing to hear a young person say your name," said Beulah. "Now, this is what I said to Eskadi, but he insisted I tell you directly. About a year ago…it was more than a year because it was in the springtime…two White men came to my house. They asked if I could use some extra money. Right away I knew something was up. Why would White men come to an old Indian woman like me and want to give me money? What do they think? That I was born yesterday?"

The hundred-year-old woman glanced over the top of her glasses to see if her visitors had caught the sly reference to her old age.

"You can laugh. There's nothing wrong with being old. It isn't exactly something you can hide from. These two White men wanted to give me some money for land they said I owned on Mount Graham. It was a lot of money. Three thousand dollars, I think that's what they said."

"Why didn't you take it?"

"Don't you know anything about the Ga'an? Didn't you listen to Song Bird the other night? No one can buy, sell or own land on the Ga'an home. Who is so foolish to think that way?"

"What did you tell them?"

"I told them it wasn't for sale because no one could rightfully own it."

"Beulah, tell Kate what you told me about the two men."

"One of the men was a priest, the priest who came to the reservation once in a while."

"Was it Father McNamara?" asked Kate.

"I don't remember what he said his name was."

"Tell her about the other man, too," urged Eskadi.

"Eskadi Black Robes, you might be the tribal chairman, but you should know better than to hurry an old woman."

"I apologize," said Eskadi.

"Now, as I was saying. The other man is the reason it came back to my mind at all. I saw him at the tribal gathering."

Kate's mind focused back to that night. She'd seen only three White men at the reservation gathering. Jake Dablo, Sheriff Hanks and Dr. Bede, the scientist who was doing some government work up on Mount Graham.

"Beulah, do you remember what the other man looked like?"

"All of those White men look pretty much the same to me, and I don't see so good anymore."

"Can you tell me if he was tall or short?" asked Kate.

"He was just a little man. Short, like me. I know because he walked right next to me. He had a crooked back, and he had big thick glasses. I think he would be blind without them. If you ask me, he is a White man without a healthy spirit. He may even have a very sick spirit."

"What did he do that made you think that?"

"He didn't have to do anything. Even with my bad vision I could see his eyes didn't lead to his heart."

Beulah reached over and touched Kate's face, rubbing it gently.

"You come and visit with this old woman

again. I would like that very much, Morning Star."

"Of course I will."

"And you, mister big shot, you take care of this woman and you might find that she will take care of you. Besides, a man with a great big brain like yours needs to keep his feet on the earth once in a while. Children, there is nothing more humbling than love."

"Good-bye old woman," said Eskadi. "Thank you for the advice."

The desert glistened in the midday sun as Eskadi and Kate walked hand in hand up the path.

"What do you think of Beulah?"

"She has an angelic spirit," replied Kate.

"What do you make of her story about Father McNamara?"

"I'm not quite sure, but I know who may be able to enlighten me."

"Jake Dablo?" asked Eskadi.

"Exactly. I heard him talking with Sheriff Hanks about land up on the mountain the Catholic Church was buying. And Deputy Funke told me before he got sick that the sheriff asked him to poke around and see what he could find out from Father McNamara's housekeeper."

"What was he looking for from her?" asked Eskadi.

"Delbert said the sheriff wanted to know if the housekeeper had heard anything about the church buying land up on Mount Graham."

"There's some kind of funny business going on," said Eskadi.

"Please tell me you've got some specifics."

"You're talking to the right guy. After you delivered Beulah's foreclosure, I began snooping around. It didn't seem reasonable to me that a big law firm from Phoenix was handling such a small potatoes type of deal. The legal fees for such a tiny land sale couldn't amount to peanuts. So I went to Farrell's office and had a little chat with his secretary."

"Farrell's secretary?"

"Her name is Darla Thompson. She told me Farrell had sold thirty or forty parcels of land up on Mount Graham to a foreign corporation by the name of AIMGO. They purchased the properties and then turned right around and placed them into a perpetual land trust."

"Is that a fairly typical way of doing business?"

"I don't know, but when I told her I was the San Carlos Tribal Chairman she mentioned that several of the defaulted properties that were bought up were once owned by Apaches."

"Is there anyone else on the reservation who might know something about this?" asked Kate.

"I'll talk to Geronimo Star in the Night. He keeps a very close eye on what's going on up on Mount Graham."

"Great. Anything you can find out will be helpful, but I'm not exactly sure what we're looking for."

As Kate pulled in front of the tribal hall, she softly touched Eskadi on the hand.

"Will I see you soon?" he asked.

"I hope so."

Deputy Steele left the reservation and drove directly to Jake Dablo's trailer. A mangy puppy with a white spot on its forehead ran to greet her.

"Maybe he recognizes you." Jake's voice startled Kate.

"I don't think I've ever seen him before. He sure is a friendly pup. What's his name?"

"Sirius."

"Serious? What an odd name."

"No," laughed Jake. "Sirius. S-I-R-I-U-S, the Dog Star. It's the brightest star in the constellation Canis Major."

Jake motioned to a sun-weathered table and chairs sitting under a plastic umbrella in front of the trailer.

"Have a seat. Coffee?"

"No, I'm fine. Thanks."

"What have you heard about Delbert? Anything new?" asked Jake.

"We are still waiting to hear from the Carondelet Neurological Institute in Tucson."

"Let's hope they can figure it out," replied Jake.

A momentary quietness hung between them like an unspoken, common prayer for a good friend. Jake broke the silence.

"I don't suppose the reason you came out this

far was to talk about Delbert. What can I do you for?"

"Jake, I need your help. I think you might have some information that could be valuable to me."

Jake rubbed his knotted fingers against his forehead and grinned.

"Zeb told me you were a straight shooter. I like that. What do you need to know?"

"It's about the land deals on Mount Graham."

Jake reached into his shirt pocket and pulled out an unopened pack of cigarettes. Slowly removing the cellophane, he tapped the fresh package against the table to draw the tobacco tight against the filter. Pulling the aluminized paper cover to one side, he lightly snapped one finger against the bottom of the package until a single cigarette popped up.

"Smoke?"

Kate eyed the cigarette. Jake eyed Kate. The temptation she was feeling was tangible. Jake could practically see the years of anti-smoking propaganda racing through her mind. He also understood that she knew a cigarette might build a bridge of camaraderie between them. Jake's gentlemanly nature offered her an easy out.

"It's not for everybody."

Kate chose to build the bridge.

"What the hell. I'll try one just to see if they taste the way I remember."

A jaunty smile appeared on Jake's lips. Kate Steele was a gamer. He handed her a cigarette and a wooden match.

"You were asking about the land deals up on Mount Graham," said Jake. "What is it you think I might know that you don't?"

Deputy Steele scraped the match head across the tabletop. It flared up wildly as she brought it to the tip of her smoke. Orange-red heat pulsated on the tobacco as she drew down. She coughed against the first inhalation.

"Excuse me," she said. "They're rougher than I remembered."

"I wish I was so out of practice," said Jake. "Now what are you looking for?"

"I know you wanted Sheriff Hanks to act as a witness for you at a county planning commission meeting a while ago."

Jake took a deep drag on his cigarette. Leaning back in his chair he said nothing. Kate watched curiously as his tongue rolled across the inside of his lower lip.

"He said you had a hunch," said Kate.

"He told you that?"

"I hear things."

"Helen Nazelrod by any chance?" asked Jake.

"I like to keep my sources confidential," replied Kate.

Jake felt the magnetism of a like-minded soul stirring the chemistry of his brain.

"Of course. The importance of confidants in the business of law can't be overstated," he said. "Always keep that in mind. Now what is it you want to know?"

Deputy Steele rested her cigarette with its long pale ash hanging over the edge of the table. She removed a small notebook from her shirt pocket.

"John Farrell," she said. "Are you suspicious of him?"

"Suspicious?"

"Let me rephrase that. Is it possible that Farrell is making some land deals to benefit himself? Or, perhaps someone close to him?"

"That's a tough one to answer. On one hand I wouldn't put it past him. On the other he may just be a dupe."

Deputy Steele picked up her cigarette and tapped the ashes to the ground. She replaced it on the edge of the table without taking a second puff.

"That tells me a whole lot of nothing, Jake. Would you mind breaking it down a little further for me?"

Jake inhaled deeply. He exhaled a pair of smoke rings. They formed a set of angel wings before dissipating into the thin desert air.

"Farrell makes a lot of money."

"There's no law against that," said Kate.

"Not as long as it's made legally. Farrell has been slowly and continually making small land purchases on the mountain. I checked records at the Office of the Registrar of Deeds. They clearly show the properties involved passed through several different corporate entities before being combined into a single property."

"Seems like a lot of extra paperwork," said Kate.

"Farrell had his reasons."

"How do you know that?"

"Three times he has brought plans before the commission to have combined parcels of non-profit land trusts designated as open-deeded properties," explained Jake.

"I don't follow."

"It means the land, which in this case is held in a non-profit land trust by a foreign corporation, could be switched at any time out of the trust to anyone."

"Why would someone do that?"

"You ever hear of the game called Three Card Monte?"

"Sure, it's a slight of hand game where the dealer shows a player three cards, then turns them face down, moves them around and the player has to guess the position of a particular card. It's a shell game."

"I think Farrell might just be the pigeon. Trouble is I don't know who's running the con."

"Is it illegal to set up a land trust that can move land around between different people?" asked Kate.

"Not necessarily, but the company holding the land is a shell corporation. It's only holding is the land on Mount Graham."

"Are you talking about the AIMGO Corporation?"

"Good work, Deputy. Might I ask how you knew that?" asked Jake.

"Like I said, I like to keep my sources confidential."

"Touché."

"So what exactly do you think is wrong with the whole picture?" asked Kate.

"I suspect the corporation is either a land swindle..."

"With the Catholic Church involved?"

"Or Farrell. Inadvertently or not he may be helping someone who has plans to change the face of Mount Graham."

"Someone? Who?"

"I don't know, but there is something real odd going on here."

"Land swindles in Arizona are as common as cactus needles."

"But there isn't enough land involved to make anybody really rich," said Jake. "So there has to be a motive other than money."

Kate rapped her fingers on the table, knocking the cigarette to the ground. Jake's foot slid over and crushed it out. She knew Jake was not telling her all he knew. She did not hesitate to play a card of her own.

"Did you know shortly before Father McNamara died he went out to the reservation to see if Beulah Trees would sell her land on Mount Graham to the church?" asked Kate.

"No, I didn't. How'd you come by that

information?"

"I talked with Beulah today."

"By any chance did Farrell accompany Father McNamara on his visit?" asked Jake.

"No, but he wasn't alone. He was accompanied by the scientist who is working for the forest service up on Mount Graham. I am fairly certain that it was…"

"Doctor Bede?"

"Yes, that's right. I understand you know him," said Kate.

"Yes, I do. So does Sheriff Hanks," said Jake.

"Any ideas what Doctor Bede was doing out at the reservation with Father McNamara?"

"Maybe he was just along for the ride. From what he says he likes to get involved with local community activities wherever he does his work. I remember Bede mentioning he was a Catholic. It's not much of a stretch to assume Bede met Father McNamara after a church service. Maybe with Doctor Bede working up on Graham, he and Father McNamara got to talking about the land Beulah Trees had up there. Who knows?"

"How would Father McNamara know Beulah had land up there to begin with?" asked Kate.

"That's a question to look into. I don't know how it all fits together. And, even if it does, does it make any difference? All I know is something is going on up on the mountain. Whatever it is, it doesn't feel right to me. But, like you said, it's only a hunch."

Jake lit another cigarette. He left the pack on the table.

"Jake, it's obvious law enforcement is never far from your mind. Mind if I ask you a personal question."

"Shoot."

"Do you miss being Sheriff of Graham County?"

Deputy Steele's question blind-sided Jake like a sucker punch. People who knew him steered clear of the touchy subject fearing it might bring to the surface emotions he was assumed to have long since buried. The question seemed innocent coming from Kate. He felt a sense of relief that someone had finally asked him.

"I suppose I could say hell no. I had my time being the law in these parts and that never again, not in a million years, would I do such a job'. But that would be a big, bad lie. The truth is I do miss it. I miss being the one person people have when they've got no one else to turn to. I miss keeping the county safe for all the people, good and bad folks alike."

Jake ground his cigarette butt into the bottom of the ashtray.

"Any more questions, Deputy?"

"Not for now."

"Anything I can do to be of help, just ask."

Deputy Steele reached out to shake hands with Jake. His soft blue eyes were surrounded by roughened, age-wrinkled skin like the aura of a seasoned cowboy.   A seasoned cowboy, she reckoned, who may have been put out to pasture a little too soon.

CHAPTER FIFTEEN

The ladies from the Superstition Springs Mineral Baths and Spa, a bathhouse with a colorful past that had served the restorative needs of miners for a hundred years, were having their monthly staff meeting at the Town Talk. The owner, Mabel Larson, a gossipy but staunch upright Mormon, and her daughter, Edna Speers, a woman with a heart of gold and tongue of silver, were the only employees. So the meeting was really just an excuse to go out for breakfast and catch up on additional local gossip. They chose a booth right next to Sheriff Zeb Hanks and Deputy Kate Steele's table.

"Hello gals, coffee?" asked Doreen who filled two cups before they had a chance to answer. In a split second she turned and filled Zeb and Kate's cups.

"Sheriff," said Edna. "I understand Delbert might be coming home soon."

"Where'd you hear that? I only found out this morning myself."

"Ike Svensendorfer was in early this morning for a rub down. That skinny old goat knew all about it."

"There ain't no secrets in this town," exclaimed Doreen.

"You can say that again. We hear more gossip in the Town Talk in one day than fall on a priest's ears in a month's worth of confessions," replied Edna.

The ladies burst into a group giggle. It was a hilarious line coming from the mouth of a Mormon to the ears of Doreen and Kate, former Catholic schoolgirls.

"As long as we aren't hiding any secrets…Sheriff, is it true what we've heard about your department investigating Father McNamara's so-called suicide?"

"What?" exclaimed Doreen, sitting up quickly. "I've knowed all along that Father McNamara's death wasn't a suicide. Zeb, why didn't you tell me? Kate, why didn't you tell me?"

"Edna, there is no official ongoing investigation of his death," said Zeb. "What have you heard?"

"Nearly every single day we hear talk that the death of Father McNamara was no accident," said Edna.

"You're right about that," said Kate. "Unfortunately, it was no accident. It was ruled a suicide."

"That's not the word we hear," said Edna. "Word around the spa is…"

"Edna, you know what you heard is just rumors and nothing more," interrupted Mabel. "When you hear something, you have to consider the source. And you should think before you go talking in front of people who were close to him."

"I sure am sorry about your priest, Doe. I know you had been spending some time over there, but

I've heard things from more than one place and lots of people are talking," said Edna.

"Go ahead, tell me what you been hearin'. It can't be no worse than hearin' everyone say he killed himself."

"Just the same, Edna's got to be careful what she says in front of a sheriff and a sheriff's deputy. Isn't that right, Sheriff?"

"If you have some information, you should share it," replied the sheriff.

"Go on now, Edna," urged Doreen.

"I'm sorry to say it in front of you, Doe, but word is Father McNamara had quite a drinking problem. And there were money problems over at Saint Barnabus."

The room became quiet as a Thursday morning church.

"You sure it's okay with you that I go on, Doreen. It doesn't get any better."

"I'm a big girl. I can take it. I know Father McNamara did like a taste of bug juice now and again. I don't think that's any big secret around this town. I've tipped one back with him myself."

"Word is that he was arrested up in Phoenix on a DUI and had to spend a night in the hoosegow."

"That was two years ago," said Doreen. "He went through treatment."

"Is the other part true?"

"What other part?" asked Doreen.

"About when he got picked up by the cops…"

"Edna, what else did you hear?" asked Doreen.

"I heard he had gambling problems too. He owed a lot of money to the Mafioso up in Phoenix."

"Now, Edna, where did you hear that?" asked Mabel.

"I heard it from the housekeeper over at the church. She told Millie Schumpert over at the bakery there were lots of papers from a law firm up in Phoenix. She happened to glance at one of them when she was straightening up. She could tell right off they had to do with some company in Italy. That's how she knew it was the mob."

"Well, now that makes sense. The Mafioso's got all that money to launder and they do it by setting up legitimate businesses. It only seems reasonable they send some of the money back to Italy. That's where the mob is from, you know. There and New Jersey," Mabel asserted with extreme authority in her voice.

"The Catholic church sent in their investigators. What were their names again? A guy and a gal…"

Everyone in the room knew that the Church had sent in its own team to investigate. In two days they had covered everyone who knew Father McNamara well. No one was privy to their conclusions, but obviously everyone had their own ideas. The usually happy expression on Doreen's face turned sour as the ladies gave the priest a good going over. The tension could have been cut with a knife. Everyone but Edna got the message.

"Here's how I got it figured," continued Edna, "Father McNamara got drunk and lost a ton of money gambling. When he sobered up, he found himself owing the Mafia big time. The Mafia controls all that stuff; gambling, prostitution. And don't forget Father McNamara had a prostitute with him when he was arrested."

"That ain't true," said Doreen angrily.

"It's the word that's going around," said Edna

"The Mafia even own a law firm up in Phoenix, you know," said Mabel.

"I even heard they run the state legislature," added Edna.

"Some say the Governor's office, too."

"President Kennedy, God rest his soul, had Mafia connections. I read that in the *Global Inquirer*, so I know it's true," said Mabel.

"Wouldn't surprise me one bit," said Edna.

Sheriff Hanks got a first-hand view of how quickly half-truths could escalate into full-blown beliefs. Facts had little relevance.

"I suppose when he didn't pay up, the Mafia had him killed. They made it look like a suicide. They know how to do that."

"I wonder how much Father McNamara could have owed the mob?" pondered Edna.

"Father McNamara may not have been perfect, but as to the women and gambling, I think I've heard just about enough," said Doreen.

"Doc Yackley said it was a suicide," said Sheriff Hanks firmly. "I was at the scene. From all the evidence we found, I have no doubt Father McNamara decided to end his own life. I'm truly sorry, Doe."

His words brought a momentary uncomfortable air of silence to the room. Mabel wouldn't let it rest.

"Some folks say the Pope himself is a member of the Mafia," said Mabel.

"These ears of mine won't stand to hear blasphemy like that," protested Doreen. "You can say what you want to about President Kennedy. He had his faults. But the Pope is the word of God on earth. The Pope is therefore infallible. He would have nothing to do with the Mafia. End of subject."

"Be that as it may, why is the Catholic Church buying all that land on Mount Graham?" asked Mabel.

"What do you know about that?" asked Deputy Steele. "What have you heard?"

Along with Zeb, Jake and Eskadi, Kale had spent hours of detective work on the case. For all their effort and in spite of all the information that was flying around the room, their conclusion was essentially the same as these ladies.

"That secretary over at the real estate office. What's her name? I can't think of it right now," said Edna. "The one that works for John Farrell. She comes to the bathhouse once a month. First Tuesday of every month. Just like clockwork."

"Darla Thompson," said Mabel. "*Miss* Darla

Thompson."

"That's right. She's never been married. She doesn't have a soul to share her woes with. Not that what she says is so interesting. All she wants to talk about is her work. I mean really, secretary at a real estate office, how boring is that?"

All five feet and two hundred twenty pounds of Edna came alive as she threw herself into the new gossip.

"She tells me her boss, John Farrell, is selling land right and left off the top of Mount Graham. He claims he can take any property from on top of the mountain, doesn't matter how big or how small, and double, even triple, his money overnight, no questions asked. Miss Thompson said there's this property company, an international company from Italy, in Europe, where the Mafioso is from, that wants to buy every piece of land they can get their hands on and they don't care what it costs."

"I suppose it's because it's more expensive to own land in Italy," added Mabel in all seriousness. "Because the whole darn country is no bigger than a big ol' cowboy boot."

"I think it goes without saying everyone who's ever seen an Italian movie knows how crowded Rome is. Anyway, Miss Thompson starts telling me how Farrell sends her down to the courthouse to hunt and peck around for properties, properties that have been foreclosed on for back taxes. He paid her fifty dollars for every one she found.

Easy money."

Edna's captive audience was all ears.

"So Farrell buys up all those properties, doesn't pay squat for 'em. He got 'em all for the back taxes, sometimes even less from what I heard. It's common knowledge he's in cahoots with the county assessor."

"I've heard for years the county tax office works with those real estate people and lets them steal land from poor folks for next to nothin'," added Mabel.

"Like I was saying, old man Farrell buys all these properties for pennies on the dollar," said Edna. "Then he turns around and jacks up the price by a ton. This Mafioso company don't care what they have to pay. It's all laundered money anyway."

"Mind if I ask a question?" asked Sheriff Hanks.

"Go right ahead."

"Did anybody say exactly what the property is going to be used for?"

"Farrell's doing it to get rich," said Edna and Mabel in unison.

"No, I mean this Italian corporation or whatever it is."

Once again in unison the pair spoke. "The Mafioso."

"Why would anyone want to buy the top of a mountain? That doesn't make any sense."

"I can think of a lot of reasons," said Mabel.

"Like what?" asked Kate.

"Maybe a fancy resort like the ones they have up in Sedona or over in Santa Fe. We might end up being a new tourist spot for the southeastern part of the state. Or, maybe a rich guy is putting a villa up there like they have in Italy. I've seen what they look like in Sophia Loren movies."

"Or maybe the Mafia is buying it up to sell it back to the government," added Edna. "Everyone knows since Jack Kennedy was president the Mafioso and the government work together. Those Catholics are all in cahoots."

"Damn, I'll bet anything that's it," said Doreen suddenly.

"What on earth are you talking about, Doreen?" asked Zeb.

"You know the Forest Service is prowlin' all over the place up there. That funny little guy, the doctor scientist. Bede, that's his name, Dr. Venerable Bede. He's been workin' for the government for months now. He left his survey maps right there in that booth."

"What would the government want that land for? If they did want it, they could just take it by right of eminent domain anyway," mused Zeb.

"What's eminent domain?" asked Edna.

"It's a right that government has to come in and condemn a property. They can take it over for their own purposes. They do it to the Indians all the time," added Deputy Steele.

An uneasy tension overtook the room. Everyone knew of the long-standing disputes between the Mormons and the Apaches regarding that exact subject.

"We all know why they want that land," said Edna. "It's one the US Government is never going to fess up to."

"What's that?" asked Sheriff Hanks.

"UFOs."

"That's right," added Mabel.

"UFOs?" asked the sheriff.

"Yup. That's right. Even you have to admit there have been an awful lot of sightings in the Mount Graham area over the past thirty years. The number goes up every year. I can't hardly think of a soul in these parts who hasn't seen at least one. I think the government is finally going to study them."

Sheriff Hanks and Deputy Steele couldn't argue about the number of sightings. Hardly a month went by without someone claiming to have spotted a UFO near Mount Graham or at nearby Aravaipa Canyon. Some months there were as many as twenty reported sightings called into the sheriff's office. Delbert even claimed to have seen strange sky sights while on patrol in remote areas.

Deputy Steele and Sheriff Hanks were both thinking about the women's gossip on the death of Father McNamara, the sudden real estate boom on Mount Graham and the strange man by the name of Bede. Both knew there wasn't likely a kernel of truth in all the gossip. As sad as it was for Doreen to hear, Father McNamara, for reasons no one would likely ever know, had killed himself. John Farrell was simply doing his job, selling real estate. And Bede was just another temporary forest service employee doing fieldwork on Mount Graham. But Doreen knew otherwise. She had been meeting with Father McNamara once a week for months. He had been helping Doreen fight what he called a 'crisis of faith'.

But when Kate thought of Mount Graham, the holiest place in all of Apache tradition, being sold to the highest bidder, an unsettling chill flowed through her spirit. The uneasiness was accompanied by tightness in her chest that slowly extended upwards where it became a lump in the throat. What she felt was what Jake had called a lawman's uneasy hunch.

When the phone at the Town Talk rang, Doreen didn't even answer with her usual sass. The call was for Sheriff Hanks. Delbert had been released by the Neurological Institute in Tucson. He was back in the local hospital and out of extreme danger.

"I'm going to run over and have a peek at him. Deputy Steele, you've got morning rounds around town."

"Give Delbert my best. Tell him I'll be by soon to say hello."

CHAPTER SIXTEEN

Delbert looked amazingly well for a man who had been knocking on death's door only days earlier.

"Delbert, welcome home," said Sheriff Hanks.

Delbert managed a weak smile through the tube they had stuck down his throat,

"We need you to get better, Delbert," said Sheriff Hanks. "It sounds like they want to keep an eye on you for a few more days until you can go home.

Delbert managed a weak nod and the tiniest of smiles.

"Doc, what did they find over in Tucson?" asked Zeb.

"The conclusion was temporary partial respiratory paralysis. He also has an ulcer in his gut."

"Delbert? You have an ulcer? I never thought you worried about anything?" said Sheriff Hanks.

"He was poisoned somehow. They are not exactly sure what the poison was, but they should know soon."

The conversation was interrupted by Helen Nazelrod on the two-way radio strapped to Sheriff Hanks' shoulder. "Sheriff, it's John Farrell over at the Rodeo Real Estate Office. He's dead."

"Dead?"

"He hanged himself. His secretary called it in

not five minutes ago."

"What did she tell you?"

"She found him hanging by his neck inside his office when she came back from lunch. She's pretty shook up."

"I'm on my way there now."

"Sheriff, Jake just happened to walk in right after she found him. He's there now."

"Thanks, Helen."

Outside the Rodeo Real Estate building a tearful Darla Thompson was talking with Deputy Steele. Dabbing her eyes with a handkerchief, she broke into a hysterical fit of sobbing each time she tried to explain what happened.

"There he was hanging by his neck. He was dead. He was alive just an hour ago. I saw him just an hour ago. Now he's de-de-de-dead."

Sheriff Hanks nodded to his deputy as he made his way through the entrance of the two room real estate office. The outer room was little more than a busy looking secretary's desk, three wooden chairs lined neatly against the wall and a water cooler. Moving quickly Sheriff Hanks didn't see Jake Dablo crouched behind the secretary's desk looking at something on the floor. A cheap wall clock read one twenty. Next to the door leading to Farrell's office was a table with two odd looking coffee makers. Zeb glanced at the strange machines before peering around the corner into Farrell's office.

Inside, the dead body of John Farrell, hanging

by the neck, swayed ever so slightly. He stepped gingerly into the room.

"We better cut him down before anybody sees this."

Zeb, startled by the voice, turned to see Jake Dablo standing in the doorway.

"You're right."

Carefully, Zeb stood under the body. The legs of the dead man straddled his neck. Jake slipped a knife from his pocket, stood on a chair and cut him down. At once Zeb's knees buckled under the weight of the dead man. Jake did his best to help steady the load, but the awkward dead weight of John Farrell's body pushed Zeb against the desk. Both went tumbling onto the floor.

The body of John Farrell lay spread eagle on the floor. The noose was still tightly bound around his neck. The dead man's right eyelid drooped open, revealing an off center eyeball. The dried remains of a salty tear left an opaque trail from the corner of Farrell's left eye. His left arm was tucked tightly under his buttocks. The right hand, twisted into a palm up position, pointed a solitary middle finger directly to where the body had been hanging.

Overhead, the remaining portion of the rope dangled eerily. Secured to a decorative wooden beam, the rope looked like a macabre bolo tie. Jake stood back and surveyed the scene as Deputy Steele entered the room.

"Kate, is Darla okay?"

"No. Not at all. Her sister is out there consoling her now."

"Good. Kate, would you please call Doc Yackley. Ask him to come right over if he can. Then cordon off the area. I don't want anyone walking around inside the office destroying evidence."

"Yes, sir."

"Do that and come right back. I need another set of eyeballs on the scene. We've got a lot of work to do. As long as you're here, Jake, you might as well lend me a hand. You've got more experience than I do at this sort of thing."

"Glad to help."

"Helen told me Farrell's secretary came back from lunch shortly after one o'clock and found him hanging. She called the office and Deputy Steele was dispatched to the scene. She told me you were at the office when the call came in. Did she forget anything?" asked Zeb.

"That's about the way she gave it to me."

Sheriff Hanks and Jake moved methodically about the room for the better part of five minutes. They examined the dead body, the desk, the rope and the floor. Deputy Steele joined them.

"What do you make of this?" said Deputy Steele, pointing to some marks on the wooden floor.

Jake pulled his bifocals from his left shirt pocket. Kneeling down for a closer view, he noted three distinct sets of markings. Sheriff Hanks bent down and joined him, running a sole finger alongside the odd set of markings.

"These could be scuff marks from a shoe or boot," said the sheriff.

Jake raised his eyes toward the ceiling. The remaining portion of the rope that had gripped Farrell's neck and squeezed the life out of him swayed softly as a gentle desert breeze flowed through the open window. The same warm breeze caressed Kate's face as she followed the path of Jake's eyes toward the crossbeam and rope. She continued following the experienced lawman's line of vision as he stared at the recumbent body of John Farrell.

"Hush Puppies," said Jake.

Zeb and Kate exchanged a glance that set their collective minds in motion.

"Farrell is wearing Hush Puppies."

Deputy Steele eyed the heels of the dead man's shoes. Her mind reconstructed the possible course of events of Farrell's final moments as the sheriff theorized on the same subject.

"Farrell tossed a firmly tied noose over the support beam. He secured the rope with two half hitch knots to keep it from slipping." said Zeb.

"And, my guess is, he probably tugged downward on it to make certain it was secure, wanting to make certain the beam would support the weight," added Jake.

"From there one final step up onto the chair, and he stuck his head through the noose," added

Kate.

"And kicked away the chair," said Jake.

The matter of fact nature in which the men dealt with the gruesome event was a quick lesson for the young deputy. Kate quickly realized she was becoming one of them in the truest sense of her duty.

"I wonder," pondered Jake. "In that brief time after you step off the chair and before your neck snaps, does your whole life flash before you?"

"Any ideas, Deputy?" asked the sheriff.

"I took an abnormal psychology class once. We studied a chapter about people who survived attempted suicides. They all reported that life indeed slowed down and that personal memories were intensely focused," replied Kate.

"I wish we could know his last thoughts," said the sheriff. "It would go a long way in explaining his action."

"Sheriff, Jake, look over here."

Deputy Steele pointed beneath Farrell's desk to some scuff marks.

"Look at this."

The sheriff got down on his hands and knees. At first he didn't see anything.

"Do like this."

Kate tilted her head to the side.

"Look at it this way. You'll get a better angle on it."

Zeb tipped his head and brought his face close to the floor. A pair of previously unseen, intermittent, ill-defined marks on the floor became clear. His eyes followed them from beneath Farrell's desk to where they ended, directly beneath the dangling rope.

"What do you think, Deputy?"

"I think we should seal off the scene and get the body out of here. We need to check every inch of this office."

Before Zeb and Jake had a chance to comment, the booming voice of Doc Yackley filled the room.

"Zeb, what the hell is going on here? Deputy Steele called my office to report a suicide. It seems to me unnatural death is getting a little too common in these parts."

"It's John Farrell," replied Zeb. "It appears as though he's hanged himself."

Doc Yackley walked around the large desk and hovered over the body for a brief moment. Without saying a word he put on rubber gloves and began a cursory examination. He looked at his watch, checked the dead man's carotid artery, lifted his eyelids up and down, opened Farrell's mouth, stuck a finger inside and swathed the inside. He glanced in Farrell's ears and checked his hands and scalp before palpating the broken neck in great detail. After five minutes of poking and prodding he got up and walked over to the west-facing window. Pulling a pipe out of his pocket, he tapped it against the outside window ledge before filling the bowl. A few quick inhales later he spoke.

"What have you got, Zeb?"

"An apparent time of death between noon and one. Farrell's secretary left for lunch shortly before noon. He was alive then. When she returned from lunch an hour later, she found him hanging."

Doc inhaled some pipe smoke. His eyes studied the sprawled out body.

"What are you doing here, Jake?" he said turning to the ex-sheriff. "I thought you were all done with the law business."

"Just a coincidence, Doc. I happened to be…"

"Doesn't matter. Since you're here, what do you think?

"I'm not so certain," said Jake.

"I didn't think you would be."

"But then again…"

"Then again, what?" asked Doc.

"But then again, maybe…"

"Anyone care to let me in on this little cat and mouse game?" asked Deputy Steele.

"Come over here," said Doc. "I'll show you what I'm talking about."

Kneeling over the body of John Farrell, Doc Yackley carefully loosened the noose from around the dead man's neck.

"See this."

Doc pointed to the right side of the dead man's neck. The trio honed in on his instruction.

"He's got rope burns. They run the entire length of his neck. Look at these abrasions under his chin. Note two separate and distinct levels of indentation into the flesh made by the rope."

Doc carefully tipped Farrell's chin up, giving the trio a clearer view.

"Now take a look at this."

Doc opened Farrell's mouth very carefully. Using his thumb and first finger, he grabbed onto the tongue and pulled it out of the mouth.

"He bit clean through it. Twice," explained Doc. "Not once. Twice."

"What are you saying, Doc?" asked Zeb.

The old country physician relit his pipe. His nostrils flared dragonlike as smoke filtered its way out of his body.

"From my point of view, when I act as coroner of this fine county, I have to make certain all facts fit together. In this case I'm a little confused by what I see. There's no good reason for a man who hanged himself to have rope burns up and down his neck. Plus, two sets of deep indentations on the neck, well..."

"Well what?" asked the puzzled deputy.

"You want to explain it, Zeb?"

"You're doing fine, Doc."

"Deputy, I assume you're thinking Farrell stepped up on the chair, put the noose around his neck and jumped off. Right?"

"Yes, it seems that would be the logical sequence of events."

"Now take a step back for a minute. Put yourself in his Hush Puppies. Suppose you were going to hang yourself by the neck like John Farrell here decided to do. Suicide is rarely a spontaneous act. It tends to be rather well thought out. A planned act, if you will, as to time and place. I suppose his office is as good a place as any. That beam up there is a perfect spot to hang a noose. Then you would want to pick the right time. You wouldn't want to be interrupted. I guess Farrell accomplished that by waiting until lunch time when his secretary would be out of the office."

"Doc likes to think he's an amateur Sherlock Holmes," whispered Jake loud enough for all to hear. Jake tossed a wink in the direction of Deputy Steele. Unabashed by the aside, Doc Yackley continued.

"You'd toss the rope up over the beam and tighten it down hard. Wouldn't want it to slip, would you? It would be a mighty embarrassing thing if the knot came loose and you went crashing to the floor. "

The current sheriff, former sheriff and deputy all nodded in unison.

"Then you'd push a chair up underneath the rope and stick your head through the noose."

Doc paused his lecture to relight his pipe.

"Then you would cinch up the noose real good and snug and bango, kick away the chair. It's not a complicated process. Any old fool with a genuine death wish could do it."

"Sounds like you might have thought about it

once in a while yourself, Doc," said Zeb.

"I can think of better ways to leave this vale of tears. Right now, at least in this moment in time, I enjoy being among the living."

"Amen," added Jake.

"But as I was saying," said Doc, "once you kick away the chair, death comes in one of two ways. The preferable way would be a short step off the chair, a quick snap and a broken neck. You could say it would be pretty much an instant and painless departure from planet Earth."

"From the sounds of it, there's a less preferable way," said Zeb.

"I'm afraid so. The other way isn't quite so pretty. Same chair, same short step, but only now you've got a problem. The neck is a creature made of bone and sinew, and the good Lord put in a lot of fail-safe mechanisms to keep us from accidentally doing what it looks like Farrell here did on purpose. The odds are pretty good a neck is almost as tough as a bunch of tightly wound together hemp fibers."

"Are you sayin' his death might not have been instant?" asked Kate.

"I'm pretty damn sure his death was a slow time coming. Looks to me like he suffered from what has been termed the gallows struggle."

"That doesn't sound pretty, Doc," said Jake.

"I read a written description of a famous hanging over in Tombstone where a gallows struggle took place. The report said there was so much squirming, kicking and fussing about that the hanged man looked like a ticked off, hog-tied calf, about to be branded."

"Are you suggesting Farrell might have changed his mind after stepping off the chair? asked Deputy Steele.

"I can't imagine any human being, no matter how intent they were on dying, when they felt the breath of life slowly being choked out of them wouldn't reach up and grab the rope thinking that maybe they had made a mistake," said Doc.

"But the slow painful choking type of death would be damn unlikely to end up in a broken neck. If Farrell went that way, he would have reached up to grab the rope in one last attempt to save his own skin. It would only be the natural thing to do, even for a man bent on calling it quits."

Doc paused, hovering over the body.

"What we have here is a man who didn't try to stop anything. We have a man who never reached for the noose around his neck."

"How do you know for sure?" asked Deputy Steele.

Kate respected Doc Yackley, but she also knew the grizzled old country doctor was not a seasoned pathologist.

"Take a good gander at his hands, especially the fingernails. There's not a single strand of rope fiber under his nails. No rope abrasions like a man with hands as delicate as his would have from tightening the noose. There's not a single bit of forensic evidence telling me he ever held that rope in his hands. And, to complicate matters, his neck is fractured. Snapped in half. Broken like a twig off a dead tree branch."

"What were you saying about the rope burns on his neck?" asked Kate.

"You ever rope a calf?"

"No, I grew up in Tucson," said Deputy Kate Steele. "But I've been to a rodeo or two."

"You tell her, Zeb. I gotta get a drink of water. I'm a bit thirsty from all this yakking."

"I think what the Doc is getting at, and correct me if I'm wrong, Doc, when you rope a calf around the neck, it will fight against the rope. At first they fight a little out of surprise. It's like they're playing a game. Then when the animal realizes what's happening, it fights hard. The more the calf resists the more the rope burn. Right, Doc?"

"Keep going, Zeb. You sound like you know what you're talking about."

"The more times you pull on the rope, the closer you draw it up the neck of the calf. You gotta be careful so you don't break the neck or choke the animal, right Doc?"

"You got to be damn tough to break an animal's neck. Damn near as tough as you have to be to break a man's neck. Most people could never muster up the strength to do such a thing. Not unless they were as powerful as an ox or maybe if they were a bull goose loony with super strength," said Doc.

"Since Farrell's got two indentations and rope burns up and down his neck, he was either pulled or dragged by the rope when it was around his neck. Am I right, Doc?" asked Zeb.

"I'm leaning in that direction."

"How about the holes in the tongue?' asked Zeb.

"Now that sounds sort of like the thing they would cover with that fancy East Coast FBI Academy training. What do you think, Deputy Steele?"

"We were taught during violent confrontation people often bite through their tongues. There are many other circumstances causing that specific type of injury - electric shock, impact, fear, car accident. The list is endless."

"Let me make it one reason longer," said Doc.

Once again Doc tamped his pipe on the open window sill.

"If a man had the wherewithal to put a rope around his neck, climb up on a chair and jump off to hang himself, he sure as shootin' would know it was about to happen. He wouldn't be sticking his tongue out of his mouth like some sassy kid. But we've got Farrell who decides to bite through his tongue not once, but twice."

"It sounds to me like you might have a theory, Doc. Mind enlightening us?" asked Jake.

"No, not at all. I figure somebody knocked him

out. Then they put a rope around his neck and hoisted him to the ceiling. I haven't got the who or the why part figured out yet. All the commotion of dragging his body, hoisting and lifting it up would account for the tongue getting bit through twice, the rope burns and indentations on the neck."

"Well, then what about the broken neck?" asked Jake.

"That has me thinking. I can't really give you an answer on that one. I'm hoping that an autopsy will fill in some of the missing gaps."

"Doctor, I appreciate the input," said the sheriff. "I agree with you we should have an autopsy. Consider it ordered."

Doc nodded, "Can do."

"Until we know more the official cause of death will remain open. I don't want anybody else coming into this room until we've gone over it with a fine-toothed comb," said Zeb.

Doc Yackley snapped off his rubber examination gloves and stowed his equipment in his leather medical bag.

"When will you have time to do the autopsy?"

"I'll get at it ASAP. I should have some preliminary results for you tomorrow morning," replied Doc.

With that the doctor walked out the door.

"Looks like we got a mess on our hands, Deputy," said the sheriff. "Jake, would you by any chance be looking for a little bit of excitement?

Maybe a part time job?"

Jake's heart nearly jumped through his rib cage.

"Hell, yes I would."

"Welcome aboard," said Deputy Kate.

"Welcome back," said Zeb.

CHAPTER SEVENTEEN

"Deputy Steele, did you get anything from Darla that might help us?" asked Zeb.

"She seems awful surprised he killed himself," said Deputy Steele. "She specifically mentioned that he and his wife were planning on taking a trip to France next spring. It was supposed to be kind of a second honeymoon for their twenty-fifth wedding anniversary. His suicide doesn't make any sense at all to her."

"Do you think she'll be comfortable talking to us?" asked Zeb.

"She's pretty emotional, but I would bet she's willing to talk about it," said Deputy Steele. "I'll bring her in."

Deputy Steele walked outside where Darla Thompson was being consoled by her sister.

"Miss Thompson, I know it's a horrible time, but would you mind terribly if we asked you a few questions?"

Deputy Steele handed the bleary eyed secretary a fresh handkerchief.

"We can talk here. If you'd prefer, we could go down to the sheriff's office."

"Right here is fine, Deputy," said Darla.

"Call me Kate."

"If you want, we can use that little office at the end of the hall. We use it as a conference room."

"That would be fine," said Kate. "Would you

like a glass of water?"

"Please, but I'll get it myself."

"No, I'll get it," interrupted Jake.

"Miss Thompson?"

"You can call me Darla."

"Are you okay to take a few questions?" asked the sheriff.

"I'll try."

"Darla, how long have you worked for Mr. Farrell?"

"Ten years now. Actually it was ten years last March. March fifteenth. Ten long years. Oh! I don't mean that like it sounded. I meant ten years is a long time."

"Of course. What sort of things did you do for Mr. Farrell?"

"I answered the phone, typed letters and professional correspondence. I ran back and forth to the courthouse to file papers, a little bit of this and lot of that, if you know what I mean. I did whatever needed to be done. He called me his Gal Friday."

The mere mention of the nickname her boss had given her caused Darla's tears to flow again. Jake grabbed the tissue box from the middle of the table and set it in front of her. Sheriff Hanks waited until Darla had calmed down before continuing questioning her.

"Has Mr. Farrell seemed despondent or depressed lately?"

"No, never. Mr. Farrell was very happy," said

Darla. "His life was good. I just can't believe he killed himself like that."

Darla Thompson broke into a sobbing fit that rose and fell and rose again rapidly.

"I'm so sorry. It's just…"

"It's okay. If you feel like crying, go ahead and cry. It's normal you should feel that way," said Kate.

"I mean, his business was never better. His kids are all done with school. They have good jobs up in Phoenix. He gets along beautifully with his wife. He goes to church every week. He enjoys his work on the county planning commission. He just built a new addition onto his house. His life has never been better. I often heard him say just that."

"He had a good life," said the sheriff. "Could you tell us about today, starting from this morning?"

"I came to work and opened up like I always do at eight o'clock sharp. I put my things in order, like I always do, and started a pot of espresso. Mr. Farrell loves his espresso. He drinks it all day long. He says I make it as good as they do in France. He loved his trip to France. Paris, so romantic for the Farrells," she sighed.

Zeb, Jake and Kate listened to Darla's voice falter as she spoke of her dead boss in the present tense.

"Mr. Farrell arrived promptly at eight-thirty, like he always does. He was wearing his blue sport coat and brown slacks, and, of course, his brown Hush Puppies. They are the only shoes he ever wears. He claims they're the only shoes that fit his feet. He has terrible troubles with his bunions. I suppose that sort of thing isn't important though, is it?"

"Everything you can tell us is important, Darla," assured Kate.

"First of all, we went over yesterday's old business. That's what he calls it. Mr. Farrell likes to say, 'If it's from yesterday, its old business. If it's from today or for tomorrow, it's new business.' He likes to say smart things like that."

"Yes, ma'am," said Sheriff Hanks.

"Then I had him sign some things so they could go out in today's mail. The mailman comes around ten o'clock. Mr. Farrell signed some papers and gave me a list of calls to make. It was just like any other day around here. I made the calls, typed up some forms and went over the details for a few real estate closing appointments we have coming up later in the week. I make all of Mr. Farrell's appointments. I mean...I used to."

Once again the thought of what wouldn't be happening in the future brought tears to her eyes.

"You're doing very well, Darla," said Jake. "You're being most helpful. Would you care to continue and answer a few more questions? Or, would you like to wait a while?"

"I'm okay, honest. It's just that I can't believe Mr. Farrell is gone."

"It's hard for everyone who knew him," said the sheriff.

"Yes, I suppose so."

"What kind of mood was he in today?" asked Kate.

"Normal, I would say normal. He is not a real emotional man. He likes his work and his family, but he doesn't prattle on or anything like that. He likes to make business deals. That is probably what he likes best. Yes, to him there is nothing quite as much fun as making a sale and closing the deal."

"Did he have any big deals in the making?"

"No, not really. Just the usual, a couple of houses and some land, nothing out of the ordinary."

"Did he talk to anyone this morning?"

"He made some calls, business calls I assume. I don't really know to whom. He always keeps his door shut when he's talking. He likes his privacy. I don't mean he's secretive or anything like that. He just likes his privacy. He seemed busy with paperwork and business as usual. We didn't talk much today. Then around noon, like I always do, I went home for lunch. I had my usual lunch of tomato soup, a cheese sandwich and a glass of warm milk." She didn't mention the pinch of scotch she routinely added to her milk.

"Did Mr. Farrell stay in the office when you went out for lunch?"

"He didn't say he was going out, but it

wouldn't be unusual for him to stay at the office and work," explained the secretary.

"Was he in his office when you left?"

"Yes, I knocked on his door like I always do and told him I was leaving for lunch. He said like he always does, 'Enjoy the t-t-t-to−ma−to soooup.'"

Darla completely lost herself to sobbing. She began crying uncontrollably. Kate reached over and placed a hand on the weeping woman's shoulder.

"I don't know what's wrong with me," sobbed Darla. "I can't seem to stop crying."

"Tears are a way to show we care," replied Kate. "You must have thought the world of your boss. I'm sure he was a kind and decent man."

"He was. Indeed he was."

Darla began to sob again with the further realization that her boss was really gone.

"You know, it's funny what you think of at a time like this."

Darla began to shiver and shake. Then suddenly she started to laugh as uncontrollably as she had been crying only moments earlier.

"I just thought of how we, Mr. Farrell and me, used to laugh at some of the business things he did. Mr. Farrell was a good Mormon, you know. Not a ten percent tither, but a good Mormon. Me, I'm a Lutheran. 'No harm in being a Lutheran,' he used to say, 'but look out for those Catholics. They're the sneaky ones.' Oh, how we used to laugh when he said that. He said it a lot lately. Believe you me."

"What do you mean about the Catholic remark being said a lot lately, Darla?" asked Jake.

"Oh, I'm sorry. I didn't mean to offend anyone. Are you Catholic?"

"No. What I meant by my question was why did you say he had been saying it a lot *lately*?"

"Because of all the land deals up on Mount Graham. He was doing a lot of business with the Catholic Diocese. They were buying a lot of land up there this last year. I used to kid him about tithing to the Mormon Church with Catholic money. Oh Lord, how he laughed about that."

Sheriff Hanks, Deputy Steele and Jake exchanged quick glances that didn't go unnoticed by the dutiful Darla Thompson.

"Did I say something wrong?" she asked.

"No," replied Kate. "Not at all."

"Did he say what the Catholic Church was buying all the land for?" asked Zeb.

"No. Not to me anyway. I supposed it was for a retreat center for priests. Catholics are well known for doing that sort of thing. The land was in a trust, a corporate entity, I think. I don't know all the details. I don't really understand that end of the business."

"Darla, I think that's about enough for now. We're going to have to do some routine police investigative work here over the next few days. I think it will be best if no one disturbs anything here at the office."

"Well, of course," said Darla.

"So until we're done, no one should be allowed into the office," said Sherriff Hanks. "By late tomorrow I'm sure you will be able to go back in and put things in order. I don't know when Mrs. Farrell will want to come down and go through her husband's things. I'll find out when I talk to her."

At the mention of Mrs. Farrell's name, Darla once again let loose with a shower of tears.

"Is there anything you need to get out of the office before we lock it up?"

"Nothing really, just my purse and my sweater. I think that's about it."

Kate walked Darla into the office. The eerie aura accompanying death hung in the air. Darla quickly grabbed her sweater and headed for the inner office. At the doorway entrance she stopped dead in her tracks.

"My purse is in Mr. Farrell's office. I was carrying it in my hand when I found him. I remember dropping it near his desk."

Darla shivered as she peered into the room where only hours earlier she had found her boss hanging by his neck.

"There it is."

"Let me get it for you."

Kate grabbed the purse. She handed it to Darla who was staring at her employers' desk. The leather office chair remained where it had been shoved. Overhead, the rope dangled loosely, a grim reminder of the horrible event. Darla stepped to the desk and began straightening out the final papers her boss had been working on.

"Darla, please leave things as they are for now. We want to look things over. You'll have time to straighten up when the investigation is over."

"I'm sorry. Mr. Farrell likes things neat. I mop and dust the office floor every night. Cleanliness is next to Godliness. That's what Mr. Farrell says."

Darla put the papers down. As she started to walk away, she stopped and looked back at the desk.

"Now, that's odd."

"What's odd, Darla?" asked Kate.

"Mr. Farrell's espresso cup. It's missing. He always left it sitting right there on his desk. Look, you can see where it stained the desk. I could never get him to use a coaster. To be honest I gave up long ago on trying to get rid of the ring the cup left behind. The only place that cup ever went was to his mouth. I filled it when it was empty and cleaned it at the end of every day. I wonder where it went?"

"We'll have a look around for it. I'm sure it's here somewhere," assured Deputy Steele

"It's so strange. He was never at his desk without his espresso cup. Now he's gone and so is his   favorite   cup."

CHAPTER EIGHTEEN

Sheriff Hanks stood in the darkened corner of Farrell's office, studying the room as Deputy Steele walked Darla to her car. The west facing windows allowed in only a marginal amount of direct sunlight, but more than enough to fade the oak flooring around his desk. At this time of day long shadows crept steadily across the room.

The top of Farrell's large desk was sparsely ornamented. An ashtray, two neat piles of legalistic looking real estate papers and a desktop pen holder with two pens, hardly seemed the desk of a supposedly busy man. Opposite the desk a pair of chairs angled inward in a slightly asymmetric fashion. The chair nearest the door was much closer to the desk. The sheriff took a seat in it as Deputy Steele returned.

"Didn't Darla say that Farrell didn't have any clients this morning?"

"None by the time she left the office around noon," answered Deputy Steele.

"Does that chair seem out of place to you?" asked Zeb.

One chair completely askew with the other did seem incongruous with the otherwise fastidiously kept office. The deputy nodded.

"I'll ask Darla about it."

Deputy Steele walked around and stood behind the desk. Her eyes landed on the daily calendar.

It was full of handwritten notes. The square for the current day was unreadable due to coffee stains.

"Deputy Steele."

Jake's husky voice took her by surprise.

"I didn't mean to startle you. Did you find something?"

"He keeps a busy business calendar, but nothing he's written down hints at anything suicidal," said the deputy.

"How about murder?" asked Sheriff Hanks.

Jake and Deputy Steele turned to the sheriff who was on all fours, pointing to several small piles of wood shavings. They crouched down and joined him.

"Wood shavings," said Zeb. "Look at it from this angle."

Zeb shined a small ultraviolet flashlight onto the floor.

"Tell me what you see."

Interspersed among the wood shavings were fine rope fibers. Kate and Jake looked simultaneously toward the ceiling.

"What do you think?" asked Zeb.

"I'm thinking if a man hangs himself with a rope tied around a wooden beam, when he swings back and forth there's going to be a certain amount of rope fibers and wood shavings left behind as debris," said Jake.

"As much as this?" asked Deputy Steele.

"It does seem like quite a lot, especially

considering how smooth the finish on that beam is."

Kate gave the beam another glance. It was smooth, finished with lacquer.

"If the shavings came from the beam, wouldn't most of them have ended up on Farrell, in his hair or on his clothes?" asked Kate.

Without responding, Zeb walked from Farrell's office to the secretary's desk, picked up the phone and dialed.

"This is Sheriff Hanks. I need to talk to Doc Yackley right now."

Zeb drummed his fingers on the desk as he waited.

"Doc, I need you to check something on Farrell's body."

"I'm looking at his cadaver as we speak. What do you need?"

"Doc, did you notice any wood shavings or rope fibers on the body?"

"A goodly amount of both as a matter of fact. I suppose with the type of rope he used a lot of fibers rubbed off. The wood shavings seem a little excessive but, say isn't that beam real smooth wood? Kind of a shiny finish?"

"You bet it is. Good memory, Doc."

"It would take quite a bit of movement to shave off that much wood. He must have been swingin' back and forth like a pendulum," said Doc.

"Would you mind collecting those shavings for me?"

"It's as good as done."

"Thanks."

"Say, there's one more thing I noticed right off that I think you ought to know about," said Doc.

"What's that?" asked the sheriff.

"When I took off Farrell's shoes to examine his feet, I noticed his socks were pulled down around his ankles. It seemed odd, so I had a closer look."

Zeb listened as Doc inhaled on his pipe.

"And?"

"He had deep fingernail marks dug into his ankles."

"Does that mean anything to you?"

"Not yet. Thanks."

Zeb hung up the phone and walked back into the dead man's office. As he passed through the door he visualized the image Doc had put in his head, Farrell swinging like a pendulum. Zeb had read somewhere the human head weighs as much as a woman's bowling ball. The head would have flopped to the side atop a broken neck. Zeb's eyes moved back and forth as if he were watching Farrell's swinging body. Why would his socks be pulled down around his ankles? What did the fingernail gouges in his skin mean?

"Doc have anything to say?"

Deputy Kate Steele's voice quickly brought Zeb from his musing.

"He said there were plenty of wood shavings and rope fibers on Farrell's clothes. There was a fair amount of both in his hair too. He's keeping them for us."

Zeb glanced up at the beam and down on the floor.

"I guess now we have to decide how much is too much," he said. "Doc also found one other thing he's having a little trouble reckoning. Farrell's socks were pulled down below his ankles, and he had deep fingernail marks dug into his ankles."

"What do you make of that?" asked Kate.

"Nothing yet. I know from my days as a drunken bum that chigger bites around the ankles can cause a man to dig in pretty deep when he scratches himself. But, on the other hand, it might be something. Come down here," said Jake. "Feel this."

Kate and Zeb joined him on the floor. The fingertips on Jake's callused and gnarly hand danced ever so lightly across the floor. Kate placed her soft, smoother hand next to his, tracing the path with her fingertips.

"Rubber sole," said Jake, rubbing his thumb against his fingertips.

"Residue from a rubber sole."

Kate slowly rubbed over the area with her fingertips. Two distinct tracks, less than an inch wide each, about eighteen inches apart, ran from beneath Farrell's desk and ended directly under the dangling rope.

"Somebody sitting at that desk dragged their heels backwards from beneath the desk to right here," said Jake. "And it happened today."

"How can you say that?" asked Deputy Kate. "How can you be so specific about when they were made?"

"If they were made yesterday, or the day before, or even early this morning, they would be smudged over by the movements of Farrell's feet. If they hadn't been made today, Miss Thompson would have erased them with her mop last night."

"Jake, it sounds like you have a theory that goes beyond suicide," said Zeb.

"Let me sleep on it," said Jake. "We'll talk in the morning after we've got Doc's findings."

CHAPTER NINETEEN

Helen put Doc Yackley's call directly through to the sheriff.

"Good morning, Doc," said Zeb. "I wasn't expecting to hear from you so early this morning."

"It's not about John Farrell's autopsy," said Doc. "No, as a matter of fact, it's totally unrelated."

"What is it then?" asked the sheriff.

"Early this morning I was checking in on Delbert. I thought letting him know about the Farrell case might perk him up a little. I know that sounds strange, but people react, well, even improve, when you talk with them about something they feel passionately about. I think it stimulates the brain in ways we can't measure. You know Delbert, on the mend or not, likes to know what's going on around town."

"Yes," replied Zeb.

"Well, it's funny what will get somebody going. Maybe it was just coincidence, but once I started telling him about what happened he started trying to talk," said Doc. "At first I thought maybe the subject overexcited him. So I checked his vital signs and they were good enough. Right now he looks twice as alive as he has since he took ill. I thought you'd like to know. My gut tells me he knows something he can't quite communicate to us. It may be about the Farrell case."

"Thanks for letting me know, Doc. I'll stop by ASAP."

"That sounds like the right thing to do," said Doc. "Goodbye."

Zeb returned the phone back to its cradle. Minutes later, walking into the hospital room, he was amazed to see Delbert sitting up in bed. Color had returned to his cheeks and he was smiling.

"Delbert, you look like a million bucks," said the sheriff.

"Pgghrarh. Garrksh."

"I can't make out what you're saying, Delbert," said Zeb.

"Pgghrarhss."

Zeb could see that trying to speak was exhausting his deputy.

"Delbert, I know you're trying to speak. I'm trying my best to make it out, but I can't understand a word you're saying."

Zeb reached for a pen and paper on Delbert's table but almost instantly Delbert's eyes fluttered a few times and drifted. In an instant he was out cold. Zeb listened to the big deputy's gentle snoring for a few minutes. Doc shrugged his shoulders.

"It happens. He's been through a lot."

Zeb nodded. "Doc, would you get hold of me if Delbert tries to communicate something?"

"You got it," said Doc Yackley.

Zeb headed out the hospital door for a cup of

coffee at the Town Talk.

At the cafe he joined Deputy Kate Steele at the counter. He walked behind the counter and grabbed the pot and poured himself a cup.

"I just stopped by to see Delbert," he said. "He tried to talk."

"He must be improving," said Kate.

"What's with the long face, cowboy?" asked Doreen, bursting through the kitchen doors. "That cup of mud you're wettin' yer whistle with taste sour?"

"I was just explaining to Kate that I stopped by to see Delbert."

"How's the ol' boy doin'?"

"Doc says better. He had color in his cheeks. He tried to talk, but he couldn't get a word out of his mouth without getting exhausted," said Zeb.

"I was thinkin' about Delbert a touch ago," said Doreen.

"What were you thinking, Doreen?" asked Kate.

"When I was chattin' with Father McNamara one time, he told me a story about a sick boy. Seems as though the kid had been sicker than a dang dog for near on a year. His family went to every kind of special doctor there was. Still that boy got sicker and sicker. Pretty soon everyone, except his folks, gave up on his chances of ever gettin' better. Then one day a nurse asked his parents what made them so strong so as not to give up hope. The daddy said maybe they just hadn't found the right doctor yet. And the momma, she said that even though no one else, not even the boy's father, could see it, her boy was indeed on the mend. The mother knew her son got a little tiny bit better each time he had a visit from someone who cared. The mother said it was like counting up numbers, one at a time. Each prayer for the boy, each visit, every kind thought served to make him a little bit better. When enough of those good deeds come together, her son would be good as new."

"That's a wonderful story, Doreen," said Kate.

"Well, it got me thinkin'," said Doreen. "That maybe we got the same situation with Delbert."

"Believe me," said Zeb. "I know they are praying for him every day over at the church. Helen Nazelrod is seeing to that."

"That's all well and good. Ol' Delbert ain't gonna be none the worse from the power of prayer. But it was what the father said about the boy in the story Father McNamara told me that got me to thinkin'."

"What do you mean?" asked Kate.

"That maybe he just ain't had the right doctor yet. That maybe he ought to have a healin' done by a Medicine Man, by Jimmy Song Bird."

Zeb's and Kate's eyes lit up like someone turned on a light bulb in their heads.

"Kate, girl, think you could arrange that?"

"Let me see what I can do," said Kate. "I'm

headed out Song Bird's way this morning on official business. I'll run over and ask him. All right with you, sheriff?"

"Anything that will help Delbert is fine by me. I think it's a great idea."

"I'll be back by noon, or shortly after," said Deputy Steele.

"You don't suppose she's going to stop and see Eskadi while she's at it, do you, Doc?"

"A girl's gonna do what a girl's gonna do, sugar lamb. If she can bring back a healin' from Song Bird, everyone will the better off for it. Agreed?"

Zeb was a bit wary but held hope in his heart that Song Bird would have something up his sleeve.

CHAPTER TWENTY

The trip to the San Carlos reservation went quickly. Just as she crossed onto reservation land her cell phone rang. It was Eskadi asking when she would be arriving and telling her where to find him.

Kate pulled into the parking lot of the tribal center. Eskadi was talking to Song Bird under the shade of the old mesquite tree in front of the tribal offices. Her heart quickened as she approached Eskadi. She kissed him on the cheek in front of the medicine man. Song Bird tipped his head back slightly and gazed skyward sniffing the air.

"Sandalwood, I smell sandalwood floating in the air." Song Bird let out a peal of joyous laughter.

"I need your help," said Kate.

"What can I do for someone who has so much love in her heart?" asked the Medicine Man. "And such a serious look on her face."

"It's for Delbert. He's back from in the hospital in Tucson. He's better, but he is still sick. I know you can help him."

Song Bird listened intently as Kate brought him up to date on Delbert's condition. As she finished, the sound of a single red tailed hawk filtered through the air. A second bird and a third rapidly joined in a chorus. Their music gave Kate a sudden chill as Song Bird's countenance turned serious. Kate glanced quickly from Song Bird to Eskadi whose eyes were reading the Medicine Man's reaction. The birds' song ceased as quickly as it had begun.

"I have to prepare for the healing," announced Song Bird. "I will be at the hospital in Safford tomorrow."

With that, he got in his truck and pulled away. The midday sun reflected off Song Bird's truck, making it look like a ball of flame moving down the road.

"Don't you think it's fortuitous that Song Bird was here when I arrived?"

"He was actually the reason I called you. Didn't you get my message?" asked Eskadi.

"Only that you called. I was hoping it was because you wanted to see me."

"I do, but I would be lying if I told you that was the only reason I called. My phone call was actually about the land being sold on Mount Graham."

"What did you find out?"

"It's not what I found out but what Song Bird found out from Geronimo Star in the Night, the Medicine Man who lives on Mount Graham. He and Song Bird are great men. Unfortunately, they are a dying breed."

"Why do you say that?"

"They are the last fully trained Medicine Men on the San Carlos. Our people took it for granted there would always be great healers among us.

But, because of our collective arrogance, we may lose the true medicine way of the Apache. Geronimo Star in the Night does purification ceremonies. He has done so for just about every family on the reservation. He knows more about the sacred mountain and the way of the Ga'an than any of us."

"You said they've spoken?"

"Geronimo Star in the Night told Song Bird many different forces are working together to take away the sacred mountain from the Apache. He said the Apache Nation must unite to keep such a travesty from happening. Geronimo Star in the Night said now is the time for the people from every tribe to come together as brothers and sisters against the common enemies of all Native peoples. The issue is more than Native Americans versus the United States Government. Our complaints with the federal government are nothing in comparison to what it would mean if we lost our traditional religion, our delicate ecosystem and our autonomy as a people. This is a time of great importance for the Apache people. We must take an immovable stand."

The passion with which Eskadi spoke stirred Kate. Somewhere deep in her soul she realized the small amount of Apache blood running through her veins carried not only her dreams but the dreams of an entire nation, the Apache Nation. Eskadi's compassionate understanding of the needs of his people warmed her heart. His steadfast faith and principled belief system shifted her perception. Kate now saw him as a warrior, a leader of the people, her people.

"Both Song Bird and Geronimo Star in the Night have told me we are blessed because you have returned to the tribe."

Kate's spirit soared as she moved one step closer to understanding herself.

"Because you're an Apache and a Deputy Sheriff, a great responsibility has been given to you. Our great Medicine Men agree you are going to play a major role in saving the mountain."

CHAPTER TWENTY-ONE

Immediately upon returning from the San Carlos reservation Kate headed to the Rodeo Real Estate office. She found Jake and Zeb standing on stepladders examining the wooden beam and noose rope. An additional length of rope was lashed around Jake's waist.

"Sorry I'm late," she said.

"What did Song Bird say?" asked Zeb,

"Tomorrow he will perform a healing for Delbert at the hospital."

"He's a miracle worker as far as some folks are concerned. Maybe he's got something in his bag of tricks for Delbert," said Jake.

"How did everything else go?" asked Zeb.

"It went great. I mean, the writs were delivered," said Kate.

The enthusiasm in her voice caused Jake and Zeb to chuckle.

"I swear when you two get together you gossip like a pair of old hens," said Kate.

"Right now, we have work to do," said Zeb. "Grab that one over there."

The sheriff pointed to a ladder leaning against the wall. Kate carefully avoided contacting any of the potential evidence as she moved the ladder to the center of the room and climbed up.

"Here's what we've found. Look here and here."

Jake pointed to the spots on the edges of the squared off beam immediately adjacent to the rope. Kate stepped up a pair of rungs and leaned forward, peering downward from above the beam.

"Now look over here."

This time Jake pointed to the opposite side of the beam.

Kate climbed higher and looked over the top of the wooden beam.

"That's odd. One side of the beam has been worn away by the rope considerably more than the other."

Deputy Steele ran a finger over the splinters on the more damaged side.

"It appears that most of the wood splinters still attached are pointing toward the ceiling," said Kate.

"Good eyes, Deputy."

"Doesn't that seem a bit strange?" she asked.

"It sure as hell is odd," said Zeb. "With the rope being pulled down by the weight of a hanging man, you sure would assume the splinters would be pulled downward."

Deputy Steele watched as Jake unfastened the piece of rope tied around his waist.

"I've cooked up a little experiment."

Jake took the rope and laid it over the top of the beam. The rope was nearly identical in size and fiber width to the piece of the noose that remained around the crossbeam.

"Last night when I was lying in bed, I couldn't sleep. I kept seeing Farrell's face. I sat within ten feet of the man for the past few years at the county planning commission meetings. You get to know a man a little when you work with him like that. To be honest, I didn't think much of him one way or the other. But on more than one occasion he talked about how proud he was of his kids. That's the reason I couldn't sleep. I got to thinking about how much his family meant to him. No man in his right mind would kill himself and leave behind all that embarrassment for his family to live with. It just doesn't add up. Besides, he loved his work. A man is measured by his work and his family. I just don't believe that a man who loved his family would wrap a rope around his neck and jump off a chair to end it all."

"Maybe there were parts of him no one knew," said Kate. "Maybe he was suffering in a way no one could see."

"I suppose that's a possibility," replied Jake. "But all we really have right now is what's in front of our faces."

Jake tied the rope into a noose. He left just enough extra length dangling so the rope could easily be reached from the floor.

"You two stay on the ladders. I'm going to grab onto the rope and hang down with my body weight until my shoulders give out. You keep a close eye on the rope as it rubs back and forth over the beam," said Jake.

"You sure you don't want me to do that?" asked Zeb.

"I wouldn't want you to hurt yourself," replied Jake. "City can't afford a work comp claim."

Jake grabbed the dangling piece of rope and hoisted his feet up off the floor. Within fifteen seconds he lost his grip and banged his boot heels down hard onto the floor. Jake spit on his hands, prepping for a second attempt.

"Rope's slipperier than I thought."

"Maybe you're older than you think," said Zeb.

"Bah!"

This time Jake held on for nearly thirty seconds before his heels smacked against the floor.

"You want me to come down and hang on it?" asked Zeb.

"I'll give it one more shot. Besides Farrell and I are about the same size. You're too big."

"Okay, but don't hurt yourself. I might have trouble explaining what you were up to."

Jake grabbed the rope and pulled his feet off the floor.

"You're at one minute and holding," said Kate.

"No sense shootin' for any Olympic records," replied Jake.

"Your theory looks right, Jake."

The officers examined the markings from the rope on the crossbeam.

"Almost all of the little slivers of wood are pointing down. But there aren't nearly as many as where Farrell's rope was."

"How about on the other side?"

"It looks like there are equal amounts of wood gouging on each side."

"What's your conclusion, Deputy?" asked Zeb.

"Here's how I see it," said Kate. "Farrell's rope put wear and tear on the wooden beam in the opposite direction of weight bearing. When you compare that with our little experiment showing a downward force producing downward wear and tear, it can only mean one thing. The body was hoisted up there with a rope already around its neck. That way the rope pulling up against the beam would cause the splinters to point upward."

"Exactly the way I see it," said Zeb. "All that hoisting would cause more than enough friction of rope on wood to scrape off a ton of shavings."

"The Hush Puppies," said Kate.

"What about them?" asked Zeb.

"These drag marks."

Kate pointed to the drag marks running from under Farrell's desk to beneath the spot where he was found hanging.

"They were made from the heels of Farrell's Hush Puppies."

"I think you're onto something, Deputy. If Farrell was at his desk and someone put the rope around his neck, dragged him back to this spot and then pulled him up, it would go a long way in explaining the direction of the drag marks made by his shoes."

"But how could somebody overpower him and

do all that? Farrell would have put up some sort of a struggle. We don't have any evidence of that," said Kate.

"He must have already been unconscious," said Jake. "That would explain it."

"But we got one major problem, don't we?" said Zeb. "Like Kate said, there are no signs of resistance. I didn't see any injury marks on Farrell. No man just gives up and lets someone put a rope around his neck and hang him."

"We've got a jigsaw puzzle with some missing pieces," said Jake. "Let's go have a little chat with Doc Yackley. Maybe an amateur sleuth can enlighten the likes of us."

Jake drove with Deputy Steele to the morgue area of the hospital. Zeb followed in his Dodge Ram truck.

"Just the trio I've been looking for."

"Greetings, Doctor Yackley."

"Deputy Steele. Gentlemen."

Doc Yackley removed the meerschaum pipe from his mouth and peered over the top of his bifocals.

"Kate, please, just call me Doc. I don't want to lose the mysticism that goes with being an old country doctor."

"It's a deal," replied Kate. "If you call me Kate."

"It looks as though I've got some good news and some bad news for you. Why don't you come in and I'll show you what I'm talking about."

They followed Doc through swinging aluminum doors and across the spotlessly clean morgue floor.

"Here, put on these face masks," said Doc. "There's always a little bit of an odor hanging onto a dead body. This one stinks a little more than most."

Donning the rubber gloves, they followed Doc to the body in single file, like school children.

"I want to show you a few things. You will probably come to the same conclusion I did. Take a look at these pupils."

Doc Yackley reached overhead and pulled an illuminated lamp close to Farrell's corpse. Using the thumb and first finger of his right hand, he spread open the eyelids of the dead man. A scalpel in his left hand doubled as a pointer. Kate blinked reflexively as the coroner placed the tip of the knife next to the dead man's eyes. Doc twitched his head to the side, signaling them to have a closer look.

"Dilated," said Doc. "Farrell's pupils are dilated. Now look at this."

Doc placed the scalpel on the table near the dead man's ear. Carefully, he closed the eyelids. Inserting a single finger into the mouth of the dead man, he rubbed slowly along the inside of the upper teeth, then toward the back of the tongue and finally under the tongue. Chunky white thick material was gathered on the tip of his fingers. He exhibited the exudate for Kate and

Jake by wagging his finger in front of their eyes.

"Gastric ruminant, known to the general public as vomit. Farrell was full of it. I gathered up almost four ounces of the stuff."

Doc placed the material into a sterile specimen container.

"You say that like you're surprised," said Zeb.

"There is no medical reason for a hanged man to toss his cookies. At least not from being hanged."

Doc pulled back the sheet covering Farrell's body, exposing him from the waist up. Incisions made during the autopsy revealed the inside of John Farrell. Carefully using a forceps, Doc retracted the muscles of the neck.

"Right here. You can see where the neck is broken. Four fractures. Quite unbelievable. Four fractures. I've never seen anything like it. This is the third, fourth, fifth and sixth vertebra of the cervical spine, the neck. All fractured. And look at this, the larynx, the windpipe, and this is the cricoid cartilage. All crushed."

Kate, Zeb and Jake weren't exactly sure what Doc was getting at.

"Now for the pièce de résistance."

Doc grabbed a large pair of forceps. He pulled the skin away from the chest wall. The exposed rib cage had been cut and the ribs removed, leaving a five-inch hole in Farrell's chest.

"You're probably wondering how I made such a perfect cut. I used a Skill Saw from Sears. Cuts through bone like a hot knife through butter."

Doc reached inside the body, pulling a gooey, pale pinkish gray matter from beneath the ribs.

"This is what a lung looks like. The goo is called viscera. This is the pleura. You've heard of pleurisy. When this stuff is inflamed, you've got pleurisy. This stuff is called alveoli. It's where respiration, breathing, takes place. Technically, it's where the gaseous exchange between the lungs and the blood takes place. But here, right here, is what I want to show you. Actually, it's what you don't see that makes the difference. This is the bronchial tree, so called a tree because of the continuous branches it has. When you look at it, you should see something that resembles an upside down tree trunk with branches."

"Sorry Doc, I don't see that."

"Precisely."

The coroner jammed the lungs back into the cadaver.

"Because they are nowhere to be seen."

Removing his examination gloves, Doc Yackley lit his pipe. He casually leaned back against a steel examining table. Kate, Zeb and Jake took off their examination gloves and face masks. Following Doc's instruction, they placed them in a bin marked 'disposables.'

"You want to be a little more exact, Doc," said Zeb. "We're hardly medical students."

"Based on what I see, I'd have to state the cause of death as respiratory paralysis. That's why you didn't see what you should have seen in the lungs."

"The bronchial tree. You mean because it was missing?"

"Right."

"And what about the dilated pupils? And the vomit?" asked Zeb.

"The dilated pupils and the vomit lead me to believe he was poisoned. Pupillary enlargement is a sign of chemical toxicity. The vomit more or less confirms a consumed irritant."

"You seem pretty damn certain, Doc. Any idea what kind of poison?"

"I sent some blood and tissue samples up to a lab in Phoenix. Should have a pretty good idea of what poison it was, if it was poison, in a few days."

"You get anything else?"

"Just one more obvious thing. Farrell's socks were pulled down around his ankles. He had deep fingernail gouges in his skin just above the malleoli...the ankle bones. I'm certain they weren't made by Farrell's own hand."

"Why do you think that, Doc?" asked Jake.

"His fingernails were short. He clipped them even with the tips of his fingers. Not only did Farrell not have enough nail to gouge that deeply into himself, there wasn't any evidence of skin under his fingernails."

"We'd better have another look around Farrell's office," said Zeb. "Doc, you've been a great help."

"I'll phone you once I get the lab results," said Doc.

CHAPTER TWENTY-TWO

Darla Thompson paced back and forth frenetically outside of the Rodeo Real Estate office.

"I'm so glad you're back," she said. "I've got a real problem."

"What is it?" asked Kate.

"I just can't stand the idea of anyone seeing the office in such a messy state. I always kept it as neat as a pin. It really would be wrong for Mrs. Farrell to come in here to gather up Mr. Farrell's things, thinking her husband's last day was a messy one. Can I please go in there and clean now?"

"We're just about done. We have a couple of final things to do. Then you can go ahead and clean."

"Thank you. By the way did you find Mr. Farrell's espresso cup? It's funny but it bothers me terribly it wasn't in its usual place."

"We didn't run across it yet. Why don't you have a seat? We'll be finished in there shortly."

Kate walked back into the office to join Zeb and Jake.

"Farrell must have passed out right at his desk," said Zeb. "If he was poisoned somewhere else, we'd have more drag marks from the heels of his Hush Puppies. So, for the sake of argument, let's assume someone slipped poison in his drink, and he passed out in his chair at his desk. Then whoever gave him the poison pulled his chair back underneath the wooden beam."

"Which explains the single set of drag marks from his Hush Puppies," said Kate. "And the missing espresso cup."

"From there the killer must have tossed a rope over the top of the beam, put the rope around Farrell's neck and hoisted him up from his chair," said Zeb.

"Which makes perfect sense of the fray marks on the rope, the upward direction of the splinters and the way one side of the beam took so much more wear and tear," added Jake.

"What about the fingernail marks in his ankles?" asked Zeb.

"Dear lord," gasped Kate.

"Tell me," asked Zeb. "What?"

"The broken neck," said Kate. "Remember Doc said the type of noose around his neck wouldn't have caused the neck to break, yet it was broken in four places.

"Go on," said Zeb.

"I think the killer either pulled down hard while grabbing around the ankles thereby breaking the neck or..."

"Or what?"

"This is really gruesome. The killer grabbed onto Farrell's ankles and swung back and forth. With the amount of damage to the beam and all the splinters it really does indicate the body was swung back and forth while being pulled down on."

"Jesus," exclaimed Zeb. "If that's true, we have a very twisted killer on our hands."

"It would go a long way in explaining four fractured bones in the neck."

"Did you find the espresso cup yet?" shouted Darla Thompson.

"No, Darla. We're looking right now," said Kate.

Jake, Zeb and Kate quickly scoured the room.

"We didn't find one," explained Kate. "But if you find it when you're cleaning the office, please call us right away. Don't wash it. Don't even touch it. It might be evidence."

"His favorite cup? Evidence in a suicide? Well, I never."

CHAPTER TWENTY-THREE

Song Bird moved with ineffable intent throughout Delbert's hospital room. Except for four headdresses he placed at the foot of the bed, his mannerisms were more those of a Medical Doctor than those of a Medicine Man.

"Delbert, how are you feeling?"

The big deputy nodded and forced a smile. He blinked twice, hesitated and blinked once.

Delbert's mother, sitting by her son's side, served as his voice.

"One blink means yes and two blinks means no. I think that means no and yes. I don't know if he understands what he is trying to say."

"Not so great, huh, Delbert?" said Song Bird. "Maybe it's time to change that."

Delbert blinked once and held his eyes shut.

Song Bird walked to the window. Opening it slightly he placed a bundle of sage on a small piece of cedarwood at the edge of the sill. He struck a stick match with a thumbnail, lit the sage and began to chant. Placing his hand amidst the small stream of swirling smoke, Song Bird increased the pitch of his incantation as he collected dark oily residue on his fingertips. Song Bird walked to one side of the bed and smudged three lines on each of the sick man's cheeks and one from his forehead to the tip of his nose.

"Here. Put this on the sage."

Delbert's mother placed more herbs on top of the smoking sage. They created a filmy haze which blew into the room and coiled around her son's body.

Song Bird held an eagle feather in one hand and a piece of turquoise in the other. He began to pray and chant. At each of the four directions, the Medicine Man stopped and covered himself with a new headdress. With each new adornment, Song Bird placed a ceremonial ornament against Delbert's body. His gesticulations were intended to scatter the sickness to the four winds. As he completed his task, a nurse entered the room. The opening of the door swept the smoke out the window to the northwest, toward Mount Graham.

"What's going on here?" she demanded. "Does Doctor Yackley know about this?"

"We are helping a friend. A man who needs healing," answered Song Bird.

"You had better wait right here while I get Doctor Yackley. He's going to want to know about this!"

"What do I do now?" asked Delbert's mother.

"Pray," replied Song Bird. "Pray and meet me here tomorrow."

Delbert's mother bent down to kiss her son. When she turned around, Song Bird had gathered his things and disappeared with the smoke.

"Del, wait for me here," said his mother. "Don't move a muscle. I've got some serious praying to do."

Strolling out of the hospital and heading straight for the church, she felt the weight of the world had somehow been lifted from her shoulders.

Hours later, deep sleep and comforting dreams enveloped Delbert's mother as she slept in the chair next to her son's bed, holding his hand. It was almost noon before his stirring awoke her. She rubbed the sleep out of her eyes and focused on the Medicine Man who had returned.

Song Bird stood at the side of the sick man's bed. He laid out a small mortar bowl, a pestle and four bundles of herbs. Meticulously he removed a single stalk from each of the packages. He placed them in the bowl and began to grind the herbs into a fine powder. Taking some of the mixture and adding a drop of oil, Song Bird placed the concoction on the sick man's chest. With great delicacy he rubbed the mixture into Delbert's skin in a clockwise direction with the heel of his hand. Delbert's chest became purplish red. Song Bird walked to the opposite side of the bed, rolled Delbert slightly up on to his side and repeated the procedure on the sick man's back. The deputy remained still, unmoved. His mother prayed as Song Bird dipped his fingertips into a brackish, oily substance and shoved them deep into Delbert's nostrils.

Delbert began to cough and gyrate. His chest heaved up and down like a man gasping his last breath. Mournful guttural wails shot from his mouth. Suddenly he rolled onto his back, his pale face now strawberry red. He turned to his mother and smiled broadly.

"You had better go tell the doctor his patient is improving," advised Song Bird.

"Nurse," shouted Delbert's mother. "Nurse! He's better! My boy is better! Get Doc Yackley."

The nurse checked Delbert's pulse and placed her hand on his forehead.

"I'll get the doctor right away."

Doc Yackley greeted Song Bird and the happy mother before looking into his patient's eyes. Lightly touching the purplish red patches on his chest, he wiped some residue from Delbert's nose.

"Nurse, help me remove the ventilation tube," said Doc Yackley. "He's breathing on his own. Anyone care to tell me what's been going on here?"

"This man was poisoned by water hemlock," said Song Bird.

"How do you know that?" asked Doc.

"It is the job of an Apache Medicine Man to know such things. I have seen it many times. Nature gave me the cure."

"I don't know what the hell you did, but whatever it was it ranks up there somewhere between spontaneous healing and a full blown miracle. I've never been one to argue with positive results. Nurse, check Delbert's vitals every fifteen minutes and keep me informed."

"Yes, Doctor."

"Mrs. Funke, it looks as if your prayers have been answered."

The old woman was staring so deeply into her son's eyes she didn't hear a word Doc Yackley said.

"Hemlock you say, water hemlock?"

"It smells like sour carrots when it's thrown back up," said Song Bird.

"When I pumped his stomach, it smelled just like rotten carrots. I remember it as clear as a bell."

CHAPTER TWENTY-FOUR

The once hulking frame of Deputy Delbert Funke had been reduced by illness to a gangly stick figure of his former self. Nevertheless, the sheriff's face burst into a smile as he walked into the hospital room and saw his deputy standing and looking out the window.

"Delbert! Damn but you're looking good."

"Don't kid a kidder, Zeb. I got a mirror in the bathroom."

"Let me put it this way. You're looking a might better than you did a week ago," said Zeb.

"Zeb, Sheriff Hanks I mean, Deputy Steele stopped by earlier. She brought me up to date on what's been going on. I think I have something that might help."

"Why don't you sit down, Delbert. You shouldn't be straining yourself."

Delbert sat on the edge of the bed. His breathing was heavy and labored, obviously winded from the activity.

"It's about that snooping around you wanted me to do on Mrs. Espinoza. You know, Father McNamara's housekeeper."

"What did you find out?"

"She's a real nice lady. I didn't want her to think I was spying on her. So I just kind of asked her what she thought about the way Father McNamara died."

"Yes, Delbert?"

"Well, after I asked her that question, I could've knocked her over with a feather. She blessed and crossed herself three or four times, like so."

Delbert rapidly made a backward sign of the cross on his face, aping the housekeeper's behavior.

"It was like she was trying to ward off evil spirits or something. You know, like Catholics do."

"Yes."

"Then she mumbled off a whole bunch of words in Spanish. I told her to slow down 'cause I don't habla no Española but just a little bit. Then she started talking just as fast in English. I could hardly understand a word of that either."

"Did she seem excited? Or upset?"

"Both, I guess. When I finally got to hearing what she was saying, as near as I can figure anyway, she was saying she thinks the devil came right into the priest's house on the night Father McNamara died. She says half in Spanish and half in English, the diablo, that's Espanol for devil, came and carried old Padre McNamara right down to Route tres, seis, seis, in his rocking chair and set him down in front of that big ol' semi-truck. Well, shucks, I knew right off that was just crazy talk."

"Did you ask her why she believed the devil had paid a visit to Father McNamara?"

"No. I couldn't hardly get a word in edgewise

because then she started talking about how the Pope himself was friends with Father McNamara. Talk about double loco-loco. She said Father McNamara used to get letters from the Pope. She said she saw the letters with her own eyes."

"Did she say if Father McNamara saved the letters? Are they still in the rectory?"

"Naw. I asked her that too. She says Father McNamara destroyed every single one of them right after he read them. One time she even walked in on him when he was burning one of them. She asked the padre why he would burn letters from the Pope. He said they weren't actually from the Pope, but they were from some other place in Rome. The church headquarters. I forget the name of it."

"The Vatican?"

"Yeah, that was it."

"Go on, what else did she say?"

"She was worried about Father McNamara. She figured burning letters from the Pope was probably a real big sin. You know being superstitious and all like a lot of those old Mexican Catholic women are. She figured throwing those religious papers in the fire was like giving them right to the devil. Father McNamara told her it was okay because he was just following orders."

"Following orders?"

"Dang, that's exactly what I said. Mrs. Espinoza didn't know what following orders meant, but I think I got it all figured out. I was gonna tell you that night up on the mountain when that little doctor invited you, me and Jake to dinner."

"What's your idea, Delbert? What do you think was going on?"

"You know how those Catholics like to eat their fish on Friday?"

"Yes."

"Bein' there aren't so many lakes in Arizona and there's a lake up there on the mountain, maybe the Pope was buying a lake for the Catholics to fish in."

"Thanks, Delbert," said Zeb. "I'll give it some thought. Now I think you better lay down and get some rest."

"You're right, I am a little tuckered," said Delbert, lying back down on the hospital bed. "Oh, Zeb, there was one other thing. I don't think it means anything. You remember the night the padre died?"

"Yes."

"Mrs. Espinoza said Father McNamara had a dinner guest."

"Did she say who it was?"

"She didn't know his name. She said he was a funny looking hombre, no bigger than a pepito. I think that means mouse. She said he had big thick glasses."

"Thanks, Delbert. You've been a great help. Get some rest."

"Okay, boss."

"Say, Delbert, mind if I use the phone? It's

business. I gotta call the office."

Sheriff Hanks question was greeted by a rippling snore.

"Helen, put me through to Deputy Steele, would you?"

Kate answered on the first ring.

"Sheriff, I'm glad you called. I just got a phone call from Farrell's secretary. I think she was feeling guilty for being a little short with us the other day. I told her I would drop by and have one last look around."

"That's a good idea," said Zeb. "I keep getting this vague feeling there's something we overlooked."

"I'll keep that in mind. I'm on my way over there now," said Kate.

"I'll call Doc Yackley and see if he's heard anything from the lab on Farrell's blood and tissue samples. Why don't you meet me at the Town Talk when you're done, and we'll go over everything," said Zeb.

As she drove to the real estate office, Kate's eyes were drawn westward toward the top of Mount Graham. Its thundercloud encased peaks defined the boundaries of the Indian spirit world. Up high, where the sky kissed the land, was the holy turf of ancient shrines and sacred stones. The clouds near the peaks of Mount Graham parted, revealing an aqua blue sky. As the billowy formations drifted away and separated, Kate's imagination returned to childlike eyes while she envisioned thousands of images in the slowly moving clouds.

CHAPTER TWENTY-FIVE

Inside the Town Talk, Zeb walked past a trio of old men shaking dice and took a seat near the kitchen. Doreen scampered across the room to greet him.

"Good morning, tootsy-wootsy. What's shakin' your booty this morn'?"

"Delbert's on the mend. Song Bird's medicine is working."

"Hallelujah! Praise the good Lord and the Indian spirits both," exclaimed Doreen.

"What's all this blubbering about?" asked Jake.

"Ya big galoot, dincha hear the good news?"

"What? Did you win the lottery or something?"

"Naw, but if you leave a nice tip, I'll buy me a ticket on Saturday. I heard the jackpot is up to fifty one million buckaroos."

"I'll leave the tip if you tell me the happy news."

"Zeb just told me that Delbert's improvin' like crazy. Ain't that great?"

"Now that is good news, Doe."

"Lordy, I almost forgot. I got a business to run. Coffee for the good guys?"

Doreen poured a couple of cups of fresh brew for the officers as Deputy Kate Steele walked through the door.

"Katie, I suppose you already heard about

Delbert?" asked Doreen.

"Good news travels fast."

"Anything besides a cup of mud for the likes of you two? Katie, coffee?"

"Coffee's good."

"Same here," said Zeb. "Go ahead and take care of your real customers."

"I suppose with Delbert on the mend, I've got about a week to help you solve the Farrell case?" said Jake.

"Well, Jake, even if he is out of the hospital in a week, I doubt he'll be ready to get back to work any time soon. You'd better plan on sticking around a while. Deputy Steele and I can use your help."

Jake sipped his coffee, unable to hide his joy at being able to remain on the job.

"What did you find out, Kate? Did Miss Thompson spot anything unusual while she was cleaning up?" asked Zeb.

"No, but she's still in a tizzy over the missing coffee cup. Excuse me, missing espresso cup. I figured maybe he broke it and tossed it out without telling her, so I went behind the building and had a look in the dumpster."

"Makes sense," said Jake.

"Darla walked out there with me. She pointed out where Farrell parked his car. He parked in the same spot every day. According to her no one else ever parked back there."

"How'd she get to work?" asked Zeb.

"She walked."

"Find the espresso cup?"

"No, but something else grabbed my attention. There were two parking spots next to the trash bin. Farrell's was well worn and rutted. But the other spot, the one Darla said no one ever parked in, had a fresh set of double wide tire tracks."

"Double tire tracks?" asked Jake.

"A lot of the new, fancy trucks have a second set of tires on the rear axle," said Zeb. "Somebody was probably driving through the alley and did a U-turn."

"Just thought I'd mention it," said Deputy Steele. "Did you get a hold of Doc?"

"He was busy. I left a message."

"You know, the more I think about it, good old common sense tells me it's highly unlikely Farrell would hang himself. What do we really know about him?" asked Zeb.

Deputy Steele flipped open her small notebook.

"He's well to do but not rich. He has no real debt to speak of. He's been married to the same woman, Zelda, for twenty-five years. They have two adult children. No one in the family has any arrest record. He's been the owner of Rodeo Real Estate for twenty-two years. He and Zelda liked to vacation. France was their favorite spot. They didn't really live extravagantly. He was active in civic and church organizations. Most of his friends seem to be from his business associations."

"Any known enemies?" asked Zeb.

"None that I could find," said Kate.

"Did he have any major confrontations with people on the commission or people who brought matters before it?"

"There was a mild disagreement or two along the way, but nothing hostile," said Jake. "I think when you saw his reaction to my questioning the land deals up on Mount Graham, you saw him at his most confrontational."

"For argument's sake, let's say he didn't commit suicide. Let's assume he was murdered. Somebody would have to have a reason to kill such a seemingly innocuous man," said Zeb.

"A hidden enemy? An old grudge?" questioned Kate.

"Maybe he screwed somebody over in a real estate deal?" offered Jake.

"If he was murdered, he had an enemy who wanted him out of the way, maybe even needed him out of the way," said Zeb.

"Who would gain with Farrell out of the picture?" asked Deputy Steele.

"Telephone for Sheriff Hanks." A bellowing Doreen Nightingale held up the telephone and called out in perfect mimicry of an old movie hotel bellhop. "Telephone for Sheriff Hanks. Here ya' go, honey bear," said Doreen. "It's Doc Yackley."

Zeb took the phone. He talked to Doc Yackley quietly for a brief minute before returning to the counter and his fellow lawmen.

"It was poison, all right," Zeb announced. "The

lab tests confirmed it."

"What did Doc have to say?" asked Jake.

"The lab identified something called lobelia in Farrell's system. He said around here it's called Indian tobacco or water hemlock," replied Zeb.

"I've heard of Indian tobacco. People say it tastes real bitter," said Jake.

"Doc Yackley said in small liquid doses it's used as a muscle relaxant. It can also be used to make someone sweat like crazy. He said the Apaches use it to sweat out evil spirits. Larger doses are toxic, even deadly. He said Farrell's autopsy findings, the dilated pupils, the excessive sweat stains on his clothing, the changes in the lung tissue and death due to respiratory paralysis match the signs of water hemlock poisoning to a tee."

"Did he say how much hemlock was found in his system?" asked Kate.

"Four times as much as it would take to kill a man," said Zeb.

"Only a person who was bent on killing themselves would take that much of a poison. Maybe we are looking at a suicide after all," said Kate.

"If that's the case, there's a lot of evidence that doesn't make sense. The neck burns, the broken neck, the fingernail marks that were dug into his ankles, the lack of rope fibers under the fingernails, the excessive wood shavings on the body and the floor," said the sheriff.

"Granted, but how would someone have gotten Farrell to take that much poison? At gunpoint?" asked Jake.

"Wait a second," said Kate. "Didn't Darla Thompson say Farrell drank espresso all day long?"

"Yes, but so what?" asked Zeb.

"Have you ever tasted espresso?" asked the deputy.

"No. I'm not even sure exactly what it is, other than French coffee," said Zeb.

"It's coffee steamed under high pressure. It's thick, rich and aromatic, very bitter tasting…"

"Bitter? Like water hemlock?" asked Jake.

"Espresso is so strong I'll bet it could easily hide the taste of four or five drops of lobelia."

"There's one other thing Doc told me. Something Song Bird told him about Delbert," said Zeb.

"What's that?" asked Kate.

"Doc said Song Bird told him Delbert had been poisoned with water hemlock."

"Is there anyway Doc can verify that?" asked Kate.

"The poison's been out of his system too long, but Delbert's symptoms matched up with water hemlock poisoning. Doc said if it's true there's no way to prove it."

"Now we've got two poisonings on our hands. Delbert's and Farrell's."

"Jake, what do you know about water

hemlock?"

"When I was a kid, we called it pukeweed. The ranchers called it cowbane."

"Pukeweed, water hemlock, lobelia, Indian tobacco. It'd be nice if it kept to one name," said Zeb. "Let's call it water hemlock."

"In the old days every cowboy had a story about it. The one I remember hearing is about how the dumbest calf in the herd would eat some cowbane, excuse me, water hemlock, twitch like crazy and drop over dead in a fit. I guess it was quite a sight. I even heard of calves becoming so crazed they'd run right off a cliff," said Jake.

"What does water hemlock look like?" asked Kate

"Parsnips," replied Jake.

Suddenly Jake's hand began to tremble.

"Damn it!" cried Zeb.

"What?" asked Kate.

"The answer's been right here under our noses. I know where and when Delbert was poisoned."

"Jesus, Zeb, you're right," said Jake.

"Where? When?" asked Kate.

"The night before he got sick. When we were up on Mount Graham. Jake and I were up there to look at the land the Catholic Church was buying up through Farrell's real estate office. Jake was suspicious because Farrell was trying to railroad something through the county planning commission. It turned out the land was near a place where my grandfather had taken me years ago. It was also an Apache holy place."

"So what's this have to do with Delbert's poisoning?"

"Delbert happened by on long distance patrol when we all ran into Dr. Bede," said Jake. "We were returning a briefcase he had left behind here at the Town Talk. He came across as a pathetic sort of man. You know the type, a loner, no friends. I guess you could say we sort of felt sorry for him. So when he asked us to stick around for some dinner, we did."

"I'm not sure how this ties into the poisoning. Are you saying Bede poisoned Delbert?"

"Maybe, maybe not. If he did, it might have been accidental."

"What do you mean?" asked Kate.

"He made dinner for us, like I said. We had hamburgers, potatoes, carrots and parsnips."

"Parsnips? Do you think he accidentally fed you water hemlock instead of parsnips?"

"It could have happened that way," said Zeb.

"How come you and Jake didn't get sick like Delbert did?"

"I hate parsnips. Always have. I wouldn't have put any on my plate. No, wait a minute. Bede served us. I tossed mine away when Bede wasn't looking."

"So did I," said Jake, "but I saw Delbert take a bite, make an ugly face, swallow halfway and then spit the rest out. He definitely got some in his system."

"You don't think it was an accident, do you?"

"I don't know, Kate," said Zeb. "But it is kind of hard to believe that a professional who studies plants for a living might not know a poisonous plant like water hemlock from a parsnip."

"Just because someone is book smart doesn't mean they have a corner on common sense," said Jake. "But what on God's green earth could be his motive for poisoning us?"

"I don't know. Maybe he thought we were onto something." said Zeb.

"I suppose you're certain Bede poisoned Farrell too," said Jake.

"Somebody poisoned him. It seems like water hemlock is the common thread."

"Do we know anything that connects Farrell to Bede?" asked Kate.

Jake sat quietly thinking for a minute before responding to his deputy.

"The only time I know Bede and Farrell even laid eyes on each other was at the county planning commission meeting," said Zeb.

"That was the night Farrell was trying to railroad through the conditional land use permit for the Catholic Church up on Mount Graham," said Jake. But Bede was nothing more than a casual observer. Besides if this has something to do with Mount Graham, shouldn't I be the one he was going to poison and not Farrell. After all, I was the one who was questioning the goings on up there, not Farrell. Farrell was for it."

"It's beginning to look like Bede's actions were no accident," said Kate.

"It seems hard to believe Bede is a killer," said Zeb. "Next thing we'll be saying Father McNamara's death wasn't a suicide either and Bede poisoned him too."

"This is getting stranger by the minute. This whole thing might be far more interconnected than we ever dreamed of."

"What are you talking about, Kate?" asked the sheriff.

"I delivered a foreclosure notice out on the reservation to Beulah Trees not too long ago. With the foreclosure notice were some legal documents from a law firm in Phoenix. She couldn't read the papers because her vision is poor, so she took it into the tribal offices to have Eskadi look it over. He read it and, like you, smelled a rat. He started snooping around. It turned out the Phoenix law firm was dealing with Farrell's real estate office. Their client had an open option to buy the land as soon as it went into foreclosure."

"What does that prove?" asked Jake. "Farrell handled most of the real estate transactions in the area."

"It doesn't prove anything in and of itself. Hear me out. Later I went back out to Beulah's place with Eskadi. She had told Eskadi a story and he wanted me to hear it. A while back Father McNamara visited Beulah to find out if she wanted to sell her land to the Catholic Church."

"That's what I'd call a mighty popular parcel of land."

"But what's even stranger is Beulah told me there was another man with Father McNamara. She described him as a small man with tiny hands and glasses as thick as the bottom of a coke bottle," said Kate.

"Bede."

"She said the two of them drove up there in the biggest pickup truck she had ever seen. She said it had four wheels on the back instead of two."

"Bede's truck has four rear wheels. I noticed it that night of the meeting," said Jake.

"And, in back of Farrell's office, next to his parking spot, a vehicle with a double set of rear tires had been parked," said Kate.

"I think it's time we paid Doctor Bede a little visit," said Zeb. "Kate, you track down his license number through motor vehicles. Dig up whatever background information you can get on him. We'll bring him in for questioning. Find something for me. Come on, Jake. Let's roll."

CHAPTER TWENTY-SIX

Kate's fingers tapped nervously on the Rolodex. She needed information on Bede. She needed it now. The DMV was helpful in obtaining a physical description but not much else. Any possible info from state agencies would require more time than she had. A call to the Forest Service ended in a voice mail nightmare. Thumbing through the Rolodex, her finger stopped on the name of Elaine Coburn, her former mentor at the FBI Academy.

"Elaine, this is Kate Steele."

"Hello, Kate. It's good to hear from you again."

The old friends briefly exchanged pleasantries before getting down to business.

"I need your help, Elaine. I need some information, and I need it as soon as possible."

"This is your lucky day. If there is something I can give you, it's at my fingertips as we speak. We just got a new computer system installed. I am learning how to use it, so bear with me. What do you need?"

"Do you have a Dr. Venerable Bede on file anywhere?"

"Mind telling me what you're looking for?"

"Specific information about past history of criminal activity, if there is any, that is."

"Why don't you just get it locally? That information should be available to you on a state level."

"I need the information now, not next month."

"Let me see what I can do for you. Do you have a date of birth?"

"DMV states his date of birth as December two five, nineteen forty-seven."

"Driver's license number?"

"West Virginia. 5629345."

"I'll need something to cross-reference. How about educational information?"

"He has a doctorate degree in environmental botany."

"Okay, here we go. Hmm. This is interesting. Is he about five feet six inches tall, a hundred forty pounds, poor vision?"

"That's describes him well. What was that hmm all about?"

"If the man I'm looking at on my computer screen is the same man you're talking about, he has worked with the FBI as a contract worker. We've used him as an expert witness."

"Do you know under what circumstances?"

"He testified in a murder case. The poisoning of a priest."

"What!?!"

"Your disbelief is duly noted. Here, let me read what our people say about him. There are two brief dossiers about him in this file. The first one reads as follows, 'Dr. Venerable Bede is a qualified expert in the area of botanical poisoning in both qualitative and quantitative analysis.' His Ph.D. is in the field of Environmental Botany from the Massachusetts Institute of Technology with special emphasis on plants of the southwestern United States. His dossier says he is usually available for immediate travel and should be considered a reliable and dependable witness. He has never been married, has no children, pays his taxes punctually, has no history or record of arrest and is a registered Democrat."

"It sounds like he is well thought of by the FBI."

"He's what we call a stray cat."

"What's that?"

"An oddball expert. He's one of those rare birds with a niche skill area who can be called upon at a moment's notice in unusual cases. How is he involved with your problem?"

Kate cleared her throat.

"You sound hesitant. Are you concerned about investigating someone the agency has used as an expert witness?"

"The implications crossed my mind. I mean, I doubt the FBI would like it if they had missed something significant in a person's background."

"Why *are* you looking into him?"

"He's a potential suspect in multiple poisoning cases...and murder."

"That does make it difficult."

"You said you had two dossiers. Can you read me the other?"

"I can brief you on it, but you can't use the agency as the source of this information. This is deep background from his psychological profile. This type of data is never released and is inadmissible in court. It's the in-house profile we keep on our operatives. It presents quite a different picture of your suspect. It says here that although he is a highly qualified expert in the area of environmental botany, the agency should be very reticent about using his services. It seems your man, Dr. Venerable Bede, is of questionable mental status. He's obsessed with the priesthood of the Roman Catholic Church. He has a lengthy history of attempting to gain entrance into the Catholic Order of Saint Barnabus. His attempts have always ended in rejection based on a psychological profile of obsessive compulsive behavior. Each time he was refused admission into the priesthood, he was hospitalized for mental exhaustion. There is a long history of priest mimicry, including the wearing of priest's garments, unofficial celebration of the Catholic Mass and simulation of religious sacraments.'"

"Did you say the Order of Saint Barnabus?"

"Yes. Ever heard of them?"

"Only recently. A local priest committed suicide. He was a member of the Order of Saint Barnabus."

"It might only be a coincidence, but remember the case I was telling you Bede testified in? The one with the poisoned priest?"

"Yes."

"The priest was also from the Order of Saint

Barnabus."

"That's a pretty remote coincidence," said Kate.

A lingering moment of silence floated between the teacher and her former student.

"I guess you know what you're assignment is, don't you?"

"Once a teacher, always a teacher," laughed Kate. "Anything else that looks relevant on your computer screen?"

"Just one more thing. I don't know if it will be of any assistance, but a footnote here says his first choice for postgraduate education was in the Astrophysics program at MIT, but he wasn't accepted. It appears he's done okay in botany. I'll e-mail the non-classified part of his profile to your office."

"Thanks a million, Elaine."

"One last bit of advice, Kate. If he is your man, make certain of it. Since he has worked for the agency, and if it turns out he's a murderer, somebody's head is going to roll. For the time being, please keep my name as a source of information on the q.t. Good-bye."

"Good-bye and thanks again."

Kate put her head in her hands and rubbed her eyes. Eskadi had majored in Comparative Religion at Berkeley. He might know about the Barnabites. If he didn't, he would know how to find out quickly. She didn't need the Rolodex for his number.

"I didn't know you had such an exacting

interest in the Catholic Church," said Eskadi.

"I went to Catholic school, but I never heard of the Barnabites until Father McNamara died."

"Well, Katie my dear, it just so happens I kept a lot of my old textbooks. Somewhere amongst them I have a Catholic encyclopedia. Tell me what you're looking for so I know where to begin."

"This is going to sound crazy, but I am beginning to think there is a conspiracy involving the Catholic Church, the death of John Farrell, maybe even the death of Father McNamara and it all involves–"

"Mount Graham," interrupted Eskadi.

"How did you know I was going to say that?"

"There has been a conspiracy against all of the Apaches and our rights to Mount Graham for over one hundred years. The US Government forcibly took Mount Graham from the Apaches in the 1870's. We have been fighting for return of the sacred mountain ever since. They must have something really big cooked up this time."

"Why do you say that?"

"They have chosen some very powerful allies."

"What do you know that you aren't telling me?"

"I have been doing a little investigation of my own. Ever since we talked to Beulah Trees together, something has been rubbing me the wrong way. Remember when you served Beulah with a notice concerning her land being confiscated by the government?"

"It was being sold for back taxes. That doesn't fall into the category of confiscation," said Kate.

"Call it what you will," said Eskadi. "It was being taken out of Apache hands by the powers that be. The law firm in Phoenix was handling the purchase of the land through Farrell's real estate office."

"Yes, I remember you talked with the firm in Phoenix and to Farrell's secretary."

"The land was being purchased by a dummy corporation, a business venture whose sole purpose was buying land on Mount Graham."

"I suppose you're a lawyer now, too?"

"If it was honest work, I might have become one, if for no other reason than to defend myself. Anyway, I got to thinking about the dummy corporation and figured if they were doing business in Arizona, they would have had to file public papers. I got in touch with an old friend of mine who works for the Records and Deeds Department at the state government offices. I think you're going to find this information interesting."

"What is it?"

"The dummy corporation goes by the name of AIMGO."

"The sheriff has mentioned it."

"It's an acronym for American and International Mount Graham Organization. In addition, the local Catholic Church, the University of Arizona, the German government via the Max Planck Institute and the Vatican are somehow involved. You know as well as I do when big institutions join forces, they're usually going after something big."

"Eskadi, you have no factual basis for saying that."

"Maybe not yet, but I will. Whatever is happening on Mount Graham needs the sanction of the forest service, the federal government and even the county commission."

"You might be right, but you also might be acting just a little paranoid."

"To be an Indian is to be a lot paranoid. Besides, you know how the old saying goes, just because you're paranoid doesn't mean you're not right."

"Keep snooping around and find out what you can. What about Geronimo Star in the Night or Ramon Hickman? They live up on the mountain. You told me they know everything that goes on up there. Have you talked with them?"

"If I do all your legwork for you, you are going to have to put me on the payroll."

Kate chuckled at Eskadi's suggestion. The entire town of Safford would be up in arms if the sheriff's office put an Apache with strong political views about the corruption of the White government on the payroll.

"I don't think Safford is ready for you yet. But if I ever get elected sheriff, I'll keep you in mind.

Gotta run, I've got a lot of work to do. Bye."

As she hung up the phone, Kate began putting the pieces together. Zeb and Jake would return soon with Bede and she had work to do.

An hour later Zeb and Jake's boot heels crunching against the wood floor created an echo in the quiet sheriff's office.

"Did you locate him?"

"Neither Doctor Bede nor his pickup was anywhere to be found," said the sheriff. "His campsite is still occupied. He's around somewhere."

"Did you have a look at Bede's personal belongings?" asked Kate.

"Yes, what there was of them. He travels light."

"What did you find?"

"I'm not sure. I think he might be a religious nut. The interior of his tent was made up like the inside of a church. He had a miniature altar set up, a Bible, religious icons and even a set of priest's garments. It was strange. Other than that, he had a couple of changes of clothing, some food and his records and data for the Forest Service."

"You're right about him being some kind of religious nut. I talked with an old friend at the FBI, and it turns out they're very familiar with him."

Kate brought them up to speed on the background she'd obtained about Bede from the FBI.

"He's seems like a nut case all right. But that's a far cry from proving him to be a multiple murderer. On the other hand, I think we should interview him first thing in the morning," said Jake.

"I also have some interesting information on AIMGO," said Kate. "American and International Mount Graham Organization. It's a dummy corporation put together for the sole purpose of buying up land on the top of Mount Graham. It's funded by the Vatican, the Max Planck Institute via the German government, the University of Arizona and the local Catholic Church."

"You get that information from the FBI, too?" asked Zeb.

"No, Eskadi's been digging some things up," said Kate. Zeb gave Kate a look of semi-distrust. "Don't worry, I'm running it through a filter."

"Good," said the sheriff. "Be certain about all of it."

"I will. When you were gone, Delbert called. He remembered something else about that night the three of you ate supper with Bede. When he reached into the cooler to grab a beer, he saw some plant roots and some vials of brown liquid. At the time he assumed they were part of Bede's work. Now he's wondering if they weren't poison," said Kate.

"Bede's beginning to look guiltier by the minute," said Jake. "Think about it. He's a certified expert in plant toxicology with special knowledge of plants from this area. It's damn unlikely he'd have given anyone water hemlock by accident. And, it looks like we can tie him to the death of John Farrell via the double tire tracks."

"That's a long shot," said Zeb.

"Don't forget he had dinner with Father McNamara the night he committed suicide," said Kate.

Zeb found himself wondering if he had made a major mistake by not ordering an autopsy on the deceased priest.

"First thing in the morning, we'll all go up and look for him," said Zeb. "We'll meet an hour before daylight at the office. I'll bring the coffee."

In the eastern sky, the light of a three-quarter moon greeted Zeb, Kate and Jake as they stepped out of the office. Above the glistening peaks of Mount Graham, a single star, seemingly alone in the western sky, pulsed radiantly.

"See that star?" asked Jake. "The ancient Greeks believed that star represented Thanatos."

"Thanatos?" asked Kate.

"Death," said Zeb. "Death."

CHAPTER TWENTY-SEVEN

"Sleep okay?" asked Zeb. "You look a little tired."

Kate slid into the truck's back seat. She grabbed the Styrofoam cup of steaming hot coffee from Jake.

"Two sugars and light on the cream, right? Jake handed her the fresh cups from the Town Talk's first pot of the day."

"Thanks, Jake. As to your question, Sheriff, I slept fine, just not long enough."

"Good, there's time for rest in the grave, Deputy, especially when there's work to be done," added Jake.

Zeb reached over and turned up the radio. A sad country song came blaring out. Zeb looked in the rearview mirror and saw Kate rolling her eyes as his raspy, gravely-throated passenger joined in.

"Don't like the song?" Zeb asked.

"Not my favorite, but it's all right."

"Must be the singer then?" said Jake.

"No" laughed Kate. "I was just waking up slowly and thinking about a dream I had last night."

"My grandfather liked to interpret dreams," said Jake. "He called them the windows to the soul. What did you dream about?"

"My mother."

Both men knew the details about her mother's

fatal car accident when she was a child.

"She comes to me sometimes in my dreams," explained Kate. "It is usually just before life changing events. This might sound crazy, but I think she comes to comfort me. It's almost like my mother, her spirit I mean, knows when something is about to happen."

"You want to know something?" asked Jake

"Sure."

"I don't think that's one bit strange. I believe in that sort of thing. In fact, I think the star we saw last night as we came out of the office may have influenced your dream. Thanatos may have been an omen," said Jake.

"What an odd thing to say," said Kate. "That's sounds crazier than me thinking my dead mother's spirit comes to me in dreams."

"Remember the name of the star Thanatos - death, the child of the night," said Jake. "The Ancient Greeks had a way of looking at things. In order to better understand the natural world around them, they sometimes created explanations to fit their observations. In many ways their logic makes even better sense today."

Jake's lectures on mythology were legendary around the sheriff's office. Kate had never heard one first hand.

"According to legend, Chaos was the first created person. Her children, Tartarus, Gaia and Nyx, influenced the Greeks in much the same way children influence us today. Tartarus, the God of darkness, reigned over the underworld, a horrible place where humans were punished for misdeeds on earth. Gaia, goddess of the earth, whom I believe is very similar to the Ga'an of the Apache, knows all that is done on earth. Nyx was goddess of the night, mother of Hypnos, the Fates and Thanatos. Thanatos, child of the night, death."

Kate listened carefully to Jake's story. His soft but emphatic manner and the tone of his voice struck a chord within the far recesses of her mind. Jake's voice became that of her father. She began to drift, landing in the nether world between present and past. Kate's hypnotic state of mind was suddenly snapped back to reality as Zeb slammed on the brakes.

"Christ almighty," cried Jake. "That was too damn close for comfort."

From the corner of her eye Kate caught a glimpse of a mother coyote and her three pups scampering off into the desert underbrush. Zeb slowly pulled back onto the road.

"I didn't see it coming. I wasn't watching the road. I was listening to Jake's story," said Zeb. "Sorry, I should know to be looking for animals at this time of day. Go on now, Jake, finish your story."

"To make a long story short, the Greeks firmly believed all intricacies of human existence could be foretold by looking to the sky. Life, birth, death, comedy, tragedy, war, peace and all their subtleties could be found in the stars. Seeing the bright star of Thanatos above Mount Graham last night gave me a chill that literally made the hair on my arms stand on end. When I get that feeling, I know what I'm feeling is the truth."

"That's hardly solid deductive reasoning," said Kate.

"You're right. It's hardly any kind of reasoning at all," said the former sheriff. "It has a category all its own. We learn from experience what to pay attention to and what to cast aside. That star told me something. I don't know for certain exactly what. I can't place my finger on it just yet, but I do know it concerns Bede."

"Speaking of Bede," said Kate. "How do you think he is going to react when he sees us this early in the morning?"

"I'm hoping he's still asleep," replied Zeb. "That's why I wanted to leave so early. I wanted to get up there before daybreak. If he is our man, I'd just as soon catch him off guard."

"Do you think he'll be armed?"

"We checked for guns when I was up there yesterday. There was no sign of any weapons."

"He could have one in his truck," said Kate.

"I checked out his truck too. No gun rack, no shells, nothing to indicate he's armed or even has a gun," replied Zeb. "But, just as a precautionary measure, I'll pull off the road a quarter mile before his campsite. We will approach him on foot."

The rising sun peeked over the rims of the mountaintop to the east. Thin rays of light darted through the pine trees, bouncing white-gold reflections off the wave tips on the slowly rippling surface of Riggs Lake. Zeb turned off the headlights and pulled the car to the side of the road. Kate, Zeb and Jake got out of the car, closing the doors noiselessly. In the near distance, at the edge of the campground, Bede's truck was backed into his campsite. As they cautiously approached the truck, a single dull snapping sound filtered through the air. Kate glanced toward Zeb who was loosening the cover strap on his sidearm.

"What are you doing?" whispered Kate.

The sheriff signaled silence with a finger to his lips and pointed to Kate's holster. She unloosened it.

"His truck is backed up to his campsite. The back end is loaded with his gear," said Zeb. "His tent was over there in the clearing. It's gone. He's packed to leave. He might have seen us last night and certainly would have become suspicious if he saw us rummaging through his things. Kate, you circle around about thirty feet in front of the truck and stay low as you approach. Jake you take the passenger's side. I've got the driver's side."

Kate crouched low to the ground, stopping suddenly when a dry twig snapped beneath her boot. Zeb made eye contact and hand signaled his partners to move closer to the truck. Bede was nowhere in sight. Zeb shook his head. He motioned for the lawmen to hide behind some low bushes between the truck and the road.

"He's not in the immediate vicinity. It's damn unlikely he's out counting flowers this early. Where the hell is he?"

Kate felt her heart pounding hard.

"The holy site," said Jake. "My guess is he's up there saying goodbye."

The new light of day streamed in as Zeb, Kate and Jake crept silently through the pines. Near the opening of the sacred place where the heavens meet the sky, crisp golden rays of sunlight coalesced, making the mountaintop a celestial display.

"What is this place?" whispered Kate.

Zeb responded by pointing to a ridge top where the golden light of morning glistened. Kate squinted as reflected light scattered brilliantly in all directions. Blocking out the sunlight with her hand, Kate realized what she was witnessing. It was Bede, dressed in priest's clothing, chasuble, alb and hassock, kneeling in front of a makeshift altar holding a chalice above his head. The sunlight striking the goblet sent diamond bits of refracted light into the morning sky, creating a blinding radiance.

If Bede had seen them, he gave no indication. Inching closer, the lawmen crouched to the ground as they came within earshot of Bede.

"Oh, Holy Father, all praise and glory unto you. For you are wise and kind, I sing to your name because you are sweet. Whatsoever you have ordained me to do in your name, I pray that I, your servant on earth, have accomplished all you have beseeched of me."

The lawmen crept ever closer, eyeing Bede as he took the contents of two brown vials sitting on the right hand side of the altar and poured them into the chalice. Swirling the chalice clockwise then counterclockwise with scientific precision, he created a liquid solution.

"It is of the true body and blood of the Lord Jesus Christ that I now partake."

Bede lifted a large white sacramental host in the air with the words.

"This is the body of our Lord."

Lifting the chalice, now full of liquid, he continued.

"And this is the blood of Jesus Christ."

Bede placed the communion wafer in his mouth and reached for the goblet.

"Stop!" yelled Sheriff Hanks. "Put it down."

Bolting up from his crouched position, Sheriff Hanks raced toward the would-be priest.

"No! Don't! Stop! Now!"

Unruffled by the sheriff's shouts, Bede, chalice in hand, turned from the altar and faced the oncoming deputy. From inside his vestments he calmly withdrew a gun and pointed the barrel directly at Zeb's heart.

"Bless you my son, but I have heard the call of the Lord. He wishes to see me now."

Zeb froze. Jake and Kate slowly crept their fingers toward their holstered weapons. Bede lifted the chalice to his mouth, tipped his head back and drank the contents hungrily. Turning back to the altar, he set the small handgun at the foot of the Crucifix and crumbled to the ground, clutching his stomach.

"He's poisoned himself," shouted Sheriff Hanks. "Deputy, we need to get him to a hospital. Right now!"

"Don't bother." Bede's voice was laden with finality. "It's too late. I've taken enough poison to kill ten men. I'll be dead in fifteen minutes. You can't possibly get me out of here and down the mountain in the time I have left on earth. There's nothing you can do to save me. I have chosen to die here, in this spot."

Sheriff Hanks reached down and placed a finger on the inside of Bede's wrist. His pulse raced thin and fast. The threadbare beats came with such rapidity he could barely discern one from the next. His widely dilated pupils stared back at him. Bede's face carried the look of an innocent child.

"Don't worry, Sheriff Hanks. I have commended myself into the hands of the Lord. I am not suffering. I am becoming free."

"We know what you've done," said Sheriff Hanks. "Why did you kill?"

"A dying man should never be glib, but there are many reasons why I did what I did."

Bede's voice gurgled like water being sucked down a partially clogged drain.

"A good starting point in your final investigation might be why did I try and poison you, Jake and Delbert?"

"Why indeed?" grizzled Jake angrily.

"Be careful where you place your hatred. It could kill you."

Bede's words, a strange blend of advice and admonition, fell not lightly on Jake's ears.

"Your good deputy sheriff unfortunately came across my elixirs when he retrieved a beer for himself from the cooler in my tent. Honestly, it was spur of the moment thinking. Once your deputy had seen my poison elixirs, I felt I had no choice but to get rid of all of you. It was simple logic to kill the witnesses. If your deputy hadn't interfered with the Lord's plans, I would never have acted. But I still don't understand why the lobelia didn't poison either of you."

"We didn't eat your damn parsnips. That's why," growled Jake.

"Aha, not vegetable eaters. Big men like you two eat only meat. I should have assumed that," said Bede.

"Why did you use water hemlock to try and poison us?" asked Zeb.

"Opportunity, Sheriff. Opportunity came knocking. I had just dug the water hemlock that very morning. I accidentally came across a batch of it halfway up the mountain. Dumb luck I guess. The root looks like parsnips and smells like carrots. I figured the two of you wouldn't know water hemlock from parsnips if you ate them. Your deputy must have a cast iron stomach. A mere few ounces of water hemlock is enough to kill a man. He ate twice that."

"That's where you went wrong, Bede. He swallowed half a bite and spit the rest out. He got sick, but he's going to be just fine," said the sheriff.

"Are you sure there is nothing we can do to stop you from dying?" asked Kate. "Isn't there an antidote for what you've taken? Certainly you must have thought of that."

Kate took a handkerchief from her pocket and dried the corners of Bede's mouth.

"Thank you, young woman. You are my Mary Magdalene. As to my excessive salivation, it is an unfortunate side effect of my poison."

"Indian tobacco?"

"Very good, Deputy. Very good. Yet another name for lobelia. There are many. Might I beg to ask how you came to that conclusion? An amateur botanist perhaps?"

"We know that's how you killed John Farrell. We have the lab reports."

"I suppose since my time on earth is very limited now, I should confess to his murder if for no other reason than to lighten your case load. How long has it been since I ingested the lobelia?"

"Four, maybe five minutes."

"I have no regrets about what I have done. It was preordained, out of my hands, the will of God."

Kate wiped blood and frothy saliva from Bede's mouth as he pressed his hands on his spasming stomach.

"The poison raises all hell with the gastrointestinal tract but don't worry. I'll try not to regurgitate on you."

Bede's clarity seemed almost inhuman.

"Why did you kill Farrell?" asked Zeb. "He did nothing to you."

"Allow me to tell you how, and then I'll tell you why. After all, I have only a few tales left to tell. Be so kind as to allow me to choose the order. A dying man should be granted his final wishes."

"Then tell us," said Zeb.

Bede turned momentarily to Kate. "Thank you, my dear. You know something? You are so kind. You remind me of my mother. Are you by any chance of the Catholic faith?"

The murderer's compliment and question sent an uneasy chill through Kate.

"I went to Catholic school."

"Good, good, that's good. Once again the Lord has blessed me."

"You were going to tell us how you killed Farrell?" said Sheriff Hanks.

"Yes. Pardon me, but a dying man drifts in a sea of past events. Sort of instant replay of his life," said Bede.

"How did you kill him?" demanded Jake.

"It was so simple. He was a man of routine and efficiency. I understand that kind of thinking because I too am a man of precision and competence. He ate lunch, as did his secretary, every day at the same time. Noon. I really only had to watch him twice, and ask once, to determine he would be alone in his office between twelve and one. He created the opportunity for me, really he did. His downfall was so simple. It was the fancy French coffee he loved so much. Espresso is so strong he didn't even taste the poison when he drank it. He lost consciousness in five minutes. Five minutes. How long has it been since I took my hemlock?"

"Eight minutes."

"I knew I was stronger than that fool. I took three times as much as I gave him. He was weak, but I don't hold that against him. He died valiantly. I admire that. He fought hard, or at least his body did. I cannot speak for his soul. But I get ahead of myself. After he passed out, I had to return to my truck to get the rope. I parked it in back by the garbage cans. I suppose you already know that. It hardly matters. I had already made a noose. I am a man who likes to be prepared. I was a Boy Scout, you know. Were you a Boy Scout, Sheriff?"

"Yes, Dr. Bede. I was," replied Zeb.

"That's good. Boy Scouts usually grow up to be good citizens. My mind is wandering again, isn't it? I'm sorry. I'm trying not to give in to the effects of the poison."

Bede's eyes rolled up under his eyelids. His

breathing became shallow, lessening.

"Is he dead?" asked Jake.

"I don't…"

"No, I am not dead. Just standing near Jacob's ladder. Now where was I?"

"Farrell's death, the French coffee, it was his downfall," said Zeb.

"Yes, yes. I needed to make Farrell's death look like a suicide. I thought I had succeeded. What gave me away?"

"Science, Dr. Bede. Science gave you away."

"Excellent. That's perfect. Like Christ, a Judas of my own betrayed me. Delectable irony, wouldn't you say?"

"Ironic, yes," muttered Jake.

"Go on", prompted Zeb.

"At first I put the rope around his neck as he lay slumped over his desk in the chair. Then I rolled him back a few feet and tried to throw the other end of the rope up over the beam. It wasn't long enough. It didn't reach. I stupidly tried three or four tosses before I realized I would have to throw it over the crossbeam before I put it around his neck. It's funny but I remember two thoughts I had then. The first had me wondering how I could have made such an obvious mistake with the rope. How very unscientific of me. I concluded murder is not really a logical process and therefore absolved myself immediately. The second was an old adage I had always heard. 'Give a man enough rope, and he will hang himself.' At the time I was almost unable to carry on because I found it so hilarious, the old adage I mean."

Zeb, Kate and Jake watched and listened as Bede laughed sardonically, reliving the moment. His craziness blended all too well with the effects of the water hemlock.

"Finally, I took the noose off his neck and threw it over the beam. That worked much better as it should have. I slipped the rope over his neck. He had a large Adam's apple you know. It stuck way out. Did you ever notice that about him?"

"No," said Kate.

"Yes," said Jake and Zeb simultaneously.

"I put the noose around his neck and began hoisting him with all my strength. I cut my hands. Look."

Bede held his rope-burned hands out for them to see.

"My hands felt like they were leaking blood. The Stigmata came to my mind. One prays for small miracles at times like that. I had hoped it was a direct blessing from the Lord for doing his work, but on the other hand I did not want to leave behind bloodstains. It would make my duty to God too public."

Bede paused and lifted his hands into his own line of vision.

"No, it was not Stigmata," sighed Bede. "More to the point my hands were not bleeding and John Farrell was a slightly larger man than I, so there was another problem to solve. I had to go back out to my truck and get a pair of gloves to keep the rope from slipping through my hands. The gloves worked fairly well. I was able to hoist him high enough into the air so he dangled well above the floor. I stood back and looked at him. I thought he was dead. But he started to twitch. He jerked back and forth. It seemed like he was trying to speak. I stepped nearer to have a closer look. The rope was stuck below his abnormally huge Adam's apple. The poor man was choking. I couldn't live with that. He should have died without pain. That was the idea. I do not think of myself as a brutal man. I climbed on the chair and tried to slip the rope higher up on his neck. It was troublesome and difficult. Believe me, it was an ordeal. But somehow I managed. Still he didn't die. He began squirming, kicking, twisting. He even tried to reach up toward the rope, but, in his state, his arms were too weak to reach his neck. The poison should have killed him by then. I reasoned an unintended consequence of hanging was the stimulation of the nervous system. It brought him back to life. I had to put an end to it for his sake. So I grabbed on to his ankles and pulled down hard. I actually swung back and forth a few times. It was playfully grim. Then his neck snapped like a dry tree branch. The squirming and twitching finally stopped. I then left immediately."

Kate glanced at her watch. Ten minutes gone.

If Bede were right, he had five minutes left to live.

"Why? Why did you kill him?"

"I had to. He was conspiring."

"Conspiring with whom?"

"He was buying land for AIMGO, the American and International Mount Graham Organization."

Shivering and sweating, the dying man paused and cleared his throat.

"I'm getting cold. Do you have something you could warm me with?"

Zeb took off his jacket and placed it over the trembling Bede. Kate wiped away black and green sputum from his ashen cheeks.

"Thank you both. To comfort the afflicted is an edict of the Lord. You are serving Him well."

"The conspiracy, Dr. Bede? You were talking about a conspiracy."

"The University, the Institute, the governments, the Vatican, Father McNamara, they were all working with the heretics in the Order of St. Barnabus."

"Father McNamara?"

"Yes, he had to be done away with as all Barnabites should be. The heretics of that Order shunned me repeatedly, you know."

"You killed Father McNamara?" asked Sheriff Hanks.

"Yes."

"You poisoned him too?"

"Yes, of course. I had to."

"Why?"

"Because he's a Barnabite and all Barnabites are heretics. They ruined my life and vengeance is mine, sayeth the Lord, and I, Dr. Venerable Bede, am the handmaiden of the Lord!"

Blood trickled from Bede's mouth as his words became an amalgam of saliva and sputum.

"How long since I took the poison?"

"Twelve minutes."

"Deputy, please reach into my pocket. You'll find a vial. Don't worry, it's not poison. It's Holy Oil."

Kate withdrew the glass vial from Bede's interior breast pocket and read the label.

BLESSED OIL
Saint Barnabus Church, Safford, Arizona
Blessed by Bishop O'Leary on the first Sunday of Advent

"Ironic, isn't it. I mean that I should ask you to perform Last Rites on me with Holy Oil blessed from a church whose priest I killed."

"How did the Barnabites ruin your life?" asked Zeb.

Kate pulled back, awestruck as Bede's eyes became clear and color returned to his cheeks.

"I had only one dream in my life…to become a priest. Ever since I was a child it was the one desire my mother had for me. I was groomed to be a Barnabite, to follow in the sacred steps of

Denza, first director of the Vatican Observatory."

"The Vatican Observatory," Jake whispered. "It was on Father McNamara's ring."

"I was to be the next great astronomer, but the path of my life was changed when the Barnabites refused to admit me to their Order. Unfit due to reasons of mental instability. They claimed I suffered from delusions of grandeur. They said I had a Messianic complex. They said I believed I was a direct emissary from God Almighty. I guess the joke was on them. Now the miracles I could have brought forth will never happen."

"What do you mean?"

"They are going to build the most powerful reflective light source on earth. It could have given mankind a direct source of contact with God Almighty. But only I know the secret. It is through God's ordination that I, and only I, would be able to use the power to see into His eyes. But because of their humanness, no one will be able to see into the eyes of God. The fools! They know nothing of what they have wrought."

Bede began to shake uncontrollably. His breath became a troubled, desperate wheeze. Instinctively Kate placed her hand on his shoulder. Bede shot upright into an erect position and spewed forth projectile vomit. Green gastric fluids, blood and poison flew through the air. Just as abruptly, he collapsed back onto the ground.

"Sheriff, it is time for Extreme Unction. Please, if you would."

Bede's raspy voice was barely audible. He signaled with his eyes toward the Holy Oil bottle clutched tightly in Kate's hand. She handed it to the sheriff.

"Why me?" asked Zeb. "I'm not a Catholic, I'm not a priest. I'm not…"

"Don't worry. I will guide you through the process. It is the job for a man. From the powers invested in me by God Almighty I grant you the power to give the sacrament of Extreme Unction."

Zeb knelt down next to Bede and opened the bottle of holy oil.

"Sheriff, put some oil on your fingers and repeat what I say."

Zeb poured some oil onto the tips of his fingers as instructed.

"Through this holy unction and His own most tender mercy."

Zeb repeated the prayer.

"Through this holy unction and His own most tender mercy."

"May the Lord pardon whatever sins or faults thou has committed."

"May the Lord pardon whatever sins or faults thou has committed."

"By sight. Make the sign of the cross with the Holy Oil on my eyelids."

Bede peacefully closed his eyes and didn't flutter a muscle as Zeb made the sign of the cross on his lids.

"By hearing. Anoint my ears, my nose, my

mouth and my feet when you hear my words sheriff."

"By smell."

"By taste."

"By touch."

"By walking."

Zeb anointed with holy oil the nostrils, lips, hands and feet of Bede whose breathing was becoming reedy.

"Thank you, Sheriff," whispered Bede.

Bede's body relaxed, his breathing became easy and the dilated pupils became fixed.

"My sins have been forgiven."

As the life began to ebb away from Bede's body, Zeb had one final question.

"Conspiracy, Bede. You said there was a conspiracy. Who?"

"The Barnabites, the Catholic Church, the University of Arizona, the United States Government, the German government and others."

Bede's voice trailed off and his breathing became nearly non-existent.

"Why?"

"They are going to build an astronomical observatory on sacred ground, on God's doorstep. They had to be stopped because they disobeyed God's law by disavowing me."

Bede's eyes closed as he spoke his last words.

"Now I can sleep in the stars."

Zeb felt his gentle grip become limp in his

hand. He looked at the others then back at Bede. The events caused him to shiver involuntarily. Long ago Jimmy Song Bird had taught him an Apache prayer to be said in the vicinity of Mount Graham. He recited the benediction to the spirit of the dead man as the true meaning of his final words came to light.

"Protect us from enemies and do not let harm befall us while we are near you."

CHAPTER TWENTY-EIGHT

Doreen approached Zeb, Song Bird, Jake, Eskadi Black Robes, Delbert and Kate with two pots of coffee. One was freshly brewed. The other was brown-bottomed with what looked like sludge in it. The team had gathered at the Town Talk to discuss what exactly had happened on Mount Graham. There were a thousand unanswered questions.

"Was Bede totally off his rocker? Or is there a lot more to the picture than meets the eye?" pondered Jake.

"It depends on your view of the world," replied Song Bird. "But there is much more to the story than likely will ever be known."

"I believe Bede was mentally ill," said Kate.

"Mentally ill but clever enough to plan the murders of Father McNamara and John Farrell," said Zeb.

"And smart enough to know botany like the back of his hand," added Jake.

"He knew how to poison me and Sheriff Hanks," said Delbert. "Don't forget that."

"Just because someone is mentally ill doesn't mean they are stupid or without well-planned motivation," added Eskadi.

"He was angry at the world. He felt betrayed," said Song Bird. "Bede felt as though the world, the Order of Saint Barnabus specifically, had forced him to abandon his hopes and dreams. That is powerful medicine."

Doreen filled their cups to the brim from the new pot, but not until she had poured the muck from the bottom of the nearly empty one into Song Bird's cup. They all thanked her.

"You all talkin' about that lil' dead scientist?" asked Doreen.

"Yup," replied Zeb.

"He had a nice side to him too. Don't forget that. You can never know somethin' about someone unless ya'll know everything about 'em."

"Do you know something we don't know, Doreen?" asked Zeb.

"The little fella, well, he had a sadness in his eyes. Kinda like someone who lost what was near and dear to 'em. More donuts?"

"Bring another round," said Song Bird.

Delbert licked his lips.

"I get the distinct feeling that none of this would ever have happened had the powers that be not built the telescope up on Mount Graham," said Jake. "That being said, science has made some great advances because of that telescope."

"The Apache Nation has suffered great losses because of powerful institutions that continue to destroy our way of life," said Eskadi. "Dzil Nchaa Si An belongs to the Apache people of the Apache Nation. The telescope should not be there. There is no truth greater than that."

Silence fell on the table. Everyone, even Eskadi,

knew it wasn't that simple.

"Because of John Farrell, AIMGO legally owns the land," said Zeb.

"There are powers higher than a court of law," said Eskadi.

"For now, we must rely on the court of law for justice," replied Song Bird.

"We've been in court for thirty years over our rights to Dzil Nchaa Si An," said Eskadi. "What makes you think our only option is to depend on a system that has lied to us and imprisoned us for the last two centuries."

The infinitely thoughtful Song Bird reached over and placed a calming hand on Eskadi.

"Time is on the side of the righteous. We must remain moral and honorable if we are to prevail in this long-fought battle for the mountain."

Eskadi quietly grunted with dissatisfaction while remaining respectful to his elder.

"Eskadi, it is time you truly learned the virtue of patience," said Song Bird.

"I just don't want anyone else getting hurt or killed," said Zeb.

"What happens on the mountain is a story that is far from over," said Song Bird.

"Perhaps the ending is already written in the stars," said Jake.

"Maybe the Apache Nation will write the end to the story," said Eskadi.

Zeb and Song Bird exchanged a glance. Both men knew that what had just happened was but a single chapter in a saga that would last much longer than either of them.

THE END

GET EXCLUSIVE ZEB HANKS MATERIAL
DIRECTLY FROM MARK REPS

Creating a personal relationship with my readers is one of the main reasons and inspirations for my writing. I am writing exclusive background content for my faithful readers. This will include a deep dive into the back stories of Zeb and the other characters including Echo, Jimmy Song Bird, Jake and Helen. I want you to know more about who they are and why they do the things they do. I'm also planning novellas and short stories between books. Of course, if you join the mailing list I'll let you know when my latest books are released.

It's easy to stay in touch. Sign up here to get your free content. http://eepurl.com/b6_7m-/

You can also find me and my blog on the web at www.markreps.com

Follow me on Facebook at Zeb Hanks or Twitter at @Markreps1

Mark Reps
Author ZEB HANKS: Small Town Sheriff Big Time Trouble Series

Thanks so much for reading Book 2 in the series **Zeb Hanks: Small Town Sheriff Big Time Trouble**. Check out books by Mark Reps at Amazon. https://www.amazon.com/Mark-Reps/e/B00BYFEBQ4/ref=dp_byline_cont_ebooks_1

Follow Zeb Hanks on Facebook https://www.facebook.com/zebhanks

Check out the website www.markreps.com

Follow Mark Reps on Twitter https://twitter.com/markreps1

Sign up for Zeb Hanks newsletter http://eepurl.com/b6_7m-/

I really love getting feedback from my readers, so please feel free to review any of my books on https://www.amazon.com/Mark-Reps/e/B00BYFEBQ4/ref=dp_byline_cont_ebooks_1 or www.goodreads.com

Read the first chapter of Book 3 in the series, **Ádios Ángel**, on the following pages.

ÁDIOS ÁNGEL

CHAPTER ONE

Ángel Gómez's mouth tasted like cotton. His tongue clung unnaturally to the roof of his mouth. The stabbing pain in his stomach radiated straight through to his back. His bowels rumbled, begging to be emptied. Ángel held back for fear he would once again leave the toilet bowl bloody red. Pain zinged through his throbbing head. The rank breath passing through his lips rebounded off the linoleum floor where he had fallen down drunk. His boozy dream state evoked a childhood memory of his sick, dying dog crawling into bed with him and licking his face with its final breath.

"Here, have a shot of mouthwash. It'll wake your sorry ass up." Jimmie Joe's voice boomed from every corner of the small trailer, echoing off the walls into Ángel's pain-filled ears.

Ángel slowly raised his arm toward the tequila bottle dangling in the air just beyond his outstretched fingers.

"A little hair of the dog will cure more than the memory of a bad hangover. Here, take a great big shot of this. Brand new bottle. Freshly opened. It'll calm you. I promise. Here, take it."

Jimmie Joe was insistent, demanding. As Ángel felt the coolness of the bottle in his hand, he wished he had never met, never heard of the big

White man, the one called Diablo Blanco by the Mexican brothers and tribal Apaches in the Florence State Prison. Ángel downed a swig of the cold tequila. It was cold in his hand, warm in his mouth, hot as it wormed its way down the back of his throat, burning as it splashed against the walls of his empty stomach."

"A little fire to crank your engine, eh, Ángel?"

He hated the burn of tequila but could not escape its demonic talons. Tequila was the scavenging hawk. Ángel was a helpless rabbit.

Ángel was the name his mother called him. He was her 'Angel'. He also knew that his real name, Cadete, came from his great-great grandfather, Chief Cadete Gómez. The Chief had been a Mescalero warrior who was hostile toward Americans, Mexicans and other Native American tribes. It was said Chief Cadete Gómez paid a bounty of one thousand pesos for the scalps of any enemy that crossed his path. With that heritage Ángel should have been a strong man, not weak like a child. Ironically, the name Cadete meant *volunteer*, a fact that was likely lost on the young, undereducated Cadete Ángel Gómez.

The Mescalero tribal band of native people had survived for centuries with the mescal agave as its main food staple. The White man had turned that food into booze, tequila. Tequila now ruled Ángel's life. Not that he believed it at the time, but the Native American Alcoholics Anonymous program at the state prison had taught him about how alcohol can control every aspect of a person's life. In his most sober moments he wished to regain the power over his own life. Sobriety was, however, always very short-lived for Ángel Gómez.

"Have one more, little muchacha. We have a few weeks before we have to be anywhere. We just have to sit tight and wait. We might as well have a big booze party. What do you say, little one?"

Ángel knew he had no choice. Jimmie Joe controlled him as much as the tequila did. Why not party? What the hell difference did it make?

"Does that bother you, my little muchacha? Maybe you would rather just sit here and think real hard about what it was like for the last two years, cooped up courtesy of the State of Arizona, without the comforts a man needs."

Jimmie Joe swayed the bottle hypnotically back and forth in front of the young man.

Ángel envisioned his time in prison as he downed a large swig of the toxic alcohol. The cheap tequila smelled like cat piss. It bit like a venomous snake. The damned Diablo Blanco probably cut this cheap booze with turpentine. Ángel remembered his grandfather's words. "Don't ever let the devil's drink pass your lips." He had tried to listen. But today the tequila charged his anger, twisted his mind. Ángel could hardly believe the thoughts racing through his mind once the tequila grabbed him. Screw his grandfather and his damned advice. His grandfather didn't understand. He never needed liquor, but Ángel did.

One deep, hard swig and the demons returned, this time as a group. They howled to him that his mother was burning in hell. Then they whispered a secret. Not even the Blessed Virgin would forgive him for breaking his mother's heart by running with the evil man, el hombre malo, as Ángel's fellow Mescalero Apache called Jimmie Joe.

The prison psychiatrist with his fancy suit and shiny shoes had dared to tell Ángel he must quit drinking to be a whole person, to be his true self, and most importantly to know God. Ángel wasn't even sure anymore if there was a God, except maybe the god he felt like when he drank enough alcohol. The doctor had said, "Drinking makes you paranoid, Ángel. It makes you lose control of your thinking. Alcohol makes you do crazy things." Crazy, paranoid, what was the difference? Ángel knew his grandfather had been talking to the shrink behind his back. They conspired against him. The whole world conspired against him, everyone except his lovely Juanita. Juanita and a bottle of tequila were the only two things in the world he could really count on.

His blurry eyes caught sight of the many guns Jimmie Joe had brought back to their hideout after his trip to Safford. A third, then a fourth long drink from the bottle roiled his broken, damaged spirit. Tequila made him forget about his family and the demons that roared inside his head. Newfound courage rose up inside Ángel.

"Jimmie Joe, you never said anything about guns. What do we need all these weapons for? We ain't going to shoot nobody. That's not part of the deal. You said no one would get hurt." It was false courage fueled by alcohol that propelled his words.

"Stow it," growled Jimmie Joe. "For the last time, learn to keep your mouth shut. When this thing is over, you are going to have to learn how to stay quiet and hidden or both of us are going back to jail. One of us might even end up dead."

"I'd rather be dead than back in prison."

"Careful what you wish for mi florita. Wishes have a way of coming true."

Bile raced from Ángel's stomach to his mouth as Jimmie Joe's laughter reminded him of how he managed to crawl under this rock to begin with. His first time behind bars had been the county jail. It was easy time, six months for public drunkenness and burglary. The second judge had not been so easy on Ángel when he was busted for forgery and car theft. The checks were easy to explain. They were written for cheap bottles of tequila and pills for him and his partying friends.

The nice lady social worker had written in her report that Ángel was an alcoholic and very likely cross addicted to narcotic drugs. She said in her report that he needed treatment. When the judge asked him if that was true, Ángel lied. Ángel denied having had a drink in months. He swore he never did any drugs. Drugs were for stupid people. His problems were from a head injury, a concussion he suffered as a child. Ángel claimed it was the concussion that confused his thinking and made him unclear. It was even the reason other children had picked on him. Life had not been fair to him. He pleaded for the judge to give him a break. His mother swore that every word her son spoke was the God's whole truth.

The truth was quite something else. There never had been a head injury, and Ángel was popular with almost all of the other kids his age. The car theft came after a night of revelry and boozing. He did not remember a thing about that night. He had blacked out from the booze and drugs. Ángel did not even remember being arrested after he fell asleep behind the wheel and crashed into a gas station pump.

Three years in the state prison at Florence Junction, with time off for good behavior, was something Ángel thought he could handle. He had heard the state prison had better beds and better food than the county jail. He had even heard the prisoners were better people in there. However, with his slight frame and soft features he was vulnerable. Quickly he became a target for the rapists. They called him la niña, the little girl. Ángel hated it even more than when Jimmie Joe called him mi florita, my little flower. But Jimmie Joe protected him and maybe even saved his life. It was true that Jimmie Joe beat him, berated him in front of many, but he never asked for sexual favors.

"I ain't never setting foot inside of no damn jail ever again," cried Ángel.

"That's right, hombre. Prison is a place for suckers and losers. We did our time. Now it's time we got some real money…big money."

"Tell me again how much, Jimmie Joe?"

"A million dollars, maybe even two million. More if we're lucky. And I'm feelin' mighty lucky. How about you, my little Ángel? Do you feel lucky?"

Ángel took a deep swig of tequila and grinned with happiness. Luck was running through his veins.

93611810R00168

Made in the USA
San Bernardino, CA
09 November 2018